A SHOT TO THE HEART

A Sass and Steam Novella

CATHERINE STEIN

ISBN: 978-1-949862-19-5

Book cover and interior design by E. McAuley:
www.impluviumstudios.com

For my critique group:
Bethany, Courtney, Leni, and Lyndsay. You listen, you care,
and you helped brainstorm this story to life.

And for my husband.
Thank you for the epic-first-kiss friends-to-lovers romance.

PROLOGUE

July 15, 1903

*EAR SIR,*

I cannot begin to express my appreciation for your electro-resistance therapy machine. Months ago, I suffered a grievous injury to my left arm. The doctors recommended amputation below the elbow. My father recommended a biomechanical replacement. Either would have ended my competitive archery career. I insisted I keep the arm and have it repaired as well as traditional surgery could manage.

My pleas were heard, and I am very thankful to my surgeons for all their work, but the damage to the muscles and tendons left me in danger of never regaining the strength necessary to shoot. Until I discovered your machine. Using your device, beginning on the lowest setting and working gradually, I was able to strengthen and retrain my broken limb.

Today I am shooting again.

Thanks to you, Mr. Levett, I will compete again. Thanks to you, I will prove that even the most daunting of obstacles can be overcome through grit, perseverance, and teamwork.

You are forever my teammate, and from this day forth, I share every victory with you.

Yours in deepest gratitude,
Cora Maxwell

· · · ❊ · · ·

July 19, 1903

Dear Miss Maxwell,

Thank you for your kind missive. I am utterly delighted to hear the Electro-resistance Therapeutic Muscle Stimulator has been of benefit to you. If it is not too presumptuous of me, I would love to hear further regarding the progress of your re-entry into the competitive sporting world and whether you have reaped long-term benefits from the use of the machine. It would be helpful to me both in advertising my device to the correct consumer, as well as in furthering my scientific researchings. A reply is by no means mandatory, of course. Thank you again for your kind words, and I wish you the best of luck in all your future endeavors.

Sincerely,
Adam Levett

· · · ⤺ · · ·

July 22, 1903

Dear Mr. Levett,

I would be happy to give you updates on my progress. I am hitting bullseyes at 40 yards again and hope to be up to 50 soon. I continue to use the machine to strengthen my arm.
  As for marketing your device to a wider public, might

I suggest a shorter, attention-grabbing name? Something along the lines of 'Electro-Flex'?

Regards,
Cora Maxwell

· · · ❧ · · ·

AutomaTech Home Catalog, August 1903

Electro-Flex

The all-new, fully-automated, future-tech Sports Training and Rehabilitation device.

For all ages!

Safe and Sophisticated!

Guaranteed to enhance your performance!

Tested and recommended by champion athletes!

Available via mail-order.

$6.85

1

Excerpt of a letter from Miss Cora Maxwell to Mr. Adam Levett, dated August 14, 1903

I am traveling again! Not far, only up to South Bend, but I am making plans for Chicago, Cincinnati, Cleveland, and Detroit. My aim is to compete at the Olympic Games next summer. I <u>will</u> make it!

September 1, 1904—The Louisiana Purchase Exposition and Games of the III Olympiad
St. Louis, Missouri

NO AMOUNT OF STEREOSCOPE IMAGES or raving newspaper articles could have prepared Cora for the sight of thousands—maybe millions—of electric light bulbs flaring to life in a single instant. She'd seen electric lights, of course. They were becoming ever more common in homes, and she'd been to many cities in the course of her competitive travels. She'd visited restaurants and hotels lit by electricity, and seen electric street lamps. But this...

Her gasp joined that of thousands of others. Everywhere she looked, the magic of electricity transformed the grand palaces into glittering monuments to science and technology. Lights twinkled along the rooflines. Bulbs outlined windows and doors, lit staircases and walkways, and turned the growing darkness into a quiet backdrop to their sparkling magnificence.

Levett must love this.

The thought was nothing new to Cora. Hardly a day went by when she didn't think of something that would spark his interest. Occasionally she even jotted a note in a tiny journal, so she could remember to tell him next time she wrote. It was odd, perhaps, the friendship they'd cultivated after she'd sent that note of thanks more than a year before. But she treasured the friendship no less for its unusual origins.

Another little burst of excitement bubbled through her as she gazed at the Palace of Electricity and Machinery. AutomaTech had an exhibit there. Levett had been here since July, showing off his inventions and giving demonstrations. Finally, *finally*, Cora would have the chance to meet him in person.

She had it all planned out in her head. He'd show her around the fair, introduce her to all the latest technology. She'd invite him to the athletic field to watch as she shot for gold in the archery events. And they would talk. More easily and at greater length than they ever could via letters and telegrams. They'd discuss whatever new ideas he had floating around his head right now. She'd tell him everything about her life back home and beg his advice on her potential future plans and her not-quite-but-almost fiancé.

He would help. He always helped.

Cora walked alongside the Grand Basin, mesmerized by the play of light on the surface of the water. A hard body collided with hers and she stumbled.

"Oof."

A hand caught her arm.

"Oh, I'm so sorry," she babbled, straightening up and

turning to address the person she'd crashed into in her carelessness. "I wasn't looking where—"

"No, it was my—"

Cora froze, transfixed by the intense stare of the young man looking back at her. His wavy, dark hair was a bit too long and slightly tousled. Hazel eyes peered from behind oval-shaped, wire-rimmed spectacles. His head tipped to one side, regarding her curiously. Ardently. As if she were as fascinating or as magical as the electric lights.

A fluttering filled Cora's stomach. Her skin grew warm. This handsome stranger's piercing gaze was melting her, and she wasn't sure whether it was from embarrassment or excitement.

"My fault," he finished. His hand dropped away from her arm, ending the strange connection. "Please excuse me."

"O-of course. I wasn't looking. Or, rather, I was looking at the water and the way the lights reflect."

"It's a lovely effect," he replied. "The architects did a masterful job, as you can tell. The water and the surrounding buildings work in harmony, and the placement of the lights creates an illumination that is both attractive to the eye and practical for pedestrians making their way from place to place. Provided they are looking where they are going, that is, which I wasn't. Sorry. Er, but, yes, technological marvel. The fair is full of such things." He shifted uncomfortably, breaking eye contact. "As you know, I'm sure. I should let you go. Enjoy your time here, Miss, uh… Yes. Please excuse me." He tipped his hat to her and dashed off.

Cora stared after him, wishing he would have stayed. He'd seemed nice, if a bit flustered. And she couldn't fault him for that. Not when she'd crashed into him and then gaped at him like an utter ninny with no social skills.

She wasn't usually a ninny. The social skills… well, those were far more suspect.

Cora had to give herself points for bravery. She usually did manage to speak to gentlemen who caught her eye. The things she said, however, tended to be awkward, if not inane.

"This is exactly the problem," she sighed, wandering in the direction taken by the handsome stranger who likely wanted nothing more to do with her.

Back home in Indiana, she had a perfectly nice and respectable man interested in her. Her friends and family liked Benedict. Everyone thought they made a lovely couple. But there was no spark, no zing, no "Aha!" Wasn't there supposed to be something? Everyone said when you met "the one" you just knew. Cora didn't know anything.

And then she bumped into random men and practically swooned. Which was neither a new nor an unusual occurrence. Infatuations seemed to come and go regularly these days. Which left her with a dilemma. Did she chase after someone who made her body tingle? Did she encourage the courtship of someone who didn't, hoping her feelings might change as they got to know one another? Or did she simply keep on waiting for the spark that was supposed to happen?

Cora needed a friend and confidant. Someone not from back home. Someone she could rely on to give her honest, straightforward answers. She needed Levett. Surely he'd amassed some wisdom over the years. And if he had no real advice to offer, at least he'd offer her some comfort, and an escort around the fair.

She walked on, admiring the lights and—foolishly—hoping for another glimpse of the mystery man who had bumped her.

· · · ❋ · · ·

Adam cut a swift path through the crowd on his way back to the Palace of Electricity and Machinery. With his long stride and the people leisurely enjoying the spectacle of lights, he easily created a buffer of dozens of bodies between himself and the young woman he'd embarrassed himself in front of. Dear God, could he have been more of a babbling fool?

Stop panicking. It wasn't her.

Of course it wasn't her. Cora's events were more than two weeks away. The train from Indiana was only a single day's journey, and airship travel was even faster. She had no reason to be here so soon. Besides, she would have written him of her plans.

His shoulders tensed. Maybe she had. Getting mail to him through the madness of the Exposition wasn't exactly easy. Now that he thought about it, it had been unusually long since their last correspondence.

And that's why you're imagining a random young lady to be her. In a crowd. In the dark.

True, she'd been standing right beside a lamppost, well-enough lit to see the green color of her eyes and the hint of red in her light-brown hair. But was she the same woman as in the grainy newspaper photograph of Cora he kept with her letters? Not likely. Any number of women could possess a similar shape of face and figure.

And what did it matter? She had that Benedict person back home. Or any number of possible other suitors. Not once had she said, "I am interested in you, Mr. Levett, as a romantic partner." She hadn't even implied it. They were friends. And that was fine. He'd just lock away his own silly amorous notions and continue to love her as a friend ought.

Adam ducked into the Electricity building, heading for the AutomaTech booth where his Electro-Flex was on display. Best to get back to work. Stay focused on the things he hoped to accomplish here at the Exposition.

And maybe practice what he would say when he *did* meet the real Miss Cora Maxwell in person.

2

Excerpt of a letter from Miss Cora Maxwell to Mr. Adam Levett, dated May 19, 1904

The World's Fair sounds incredible. I'm planning to give myself time to explore rather than dashing in and out just to compete. I'm sure it will be the experience of a lifetime!

Sept. 2

CORA HAD TAKEN NO MORE THAN three steps inside the Palace of Electricity and Machinery when a small metal creature skittered past her feet. It gobbled up a blob of half-melted ice cream before scurrying back to wherever it had come from.

"Cleaning rats for home and office!" called an enthusiastic voice. A man in a tweed suit wandered in Cora's direction, gesturing toward the now-clean spot on the floor. His opposite hand held a bowl of rapidly melting ice cream. "Tagget original design!" he went on. "Trusted since 1879! Accept no substitutes!"

The man flung another glob of ice cream on the floor, and the rat once again came running to clean it up.

Cora gave him a half-hearted smile and tried to continue on her way.

"With all new materials and updated technologies!"

Cora danced around him. "No, thank you." The man was a charlatan, no doubt. She was reasonably certain Tagget Industries hadn't even existed in 1879. Tagget would have been only a boy at the time. Levett would know for sure. He followed all the news about technologies and inventors. He could probably rattle off Evan Tagget's birthday, number of patents held, and personal net worth. Cora only knew what the papers said about his scandalous affairs, most of which sounded like utter nonsense. Reading lurid accounts of the scandals of famous people was one of her favorite pastimes, and over the years she'd learned how to tell which stories were probably true, which had only small bits of the truth, and which were entirely fabricated in order to sell papers. She enjoyed them all equally.

"The AutomaTech exhibit?" she asked a grim-faced man standing beside a display of electric bread-toasters. A piece of toast in one of the models was smoking. Cora wrinkled her nose at the odor. Perhaps when the cleaning rat ran out of ice cream, it could switch to burnt toast.

"Thataway. Far end of the building."

"Thank you." She gave the toaster man a little bob of her head and skipped off down the long corridor.

All throughout the building, machines buzzed, hummed, and flashed. Wires criss-crossed the ceiling and ran down the walls so devices like the toasters could plug into the electricity flowing into the building. Just how many wires were needed to power so many things at once? And what generated that much electricity? Massive steam engines? Another question for Levett.

"Cleaning rats for home and office!"

Cora picked up her skirts and jogged past a grinning saleswoman. No more demonstrations. She was here to find her friend, not to purchase the latest appliances.

Fifty yards down the hall, she at last reached the AutomaTech exhibit. A twelve foot high iron gate marked the entrance to the company's designated area. A pair of guard dragons flanked the opening, sitting on their dog-like haunches while their eagle heads swiveled back and forth, watching the fairgoers.

"Welcome to AutomaTech," a crackling recorded voice spoke. "The leader in affordable mail-order technology. Browse the AutomaTech catalog today and bring the best of automation into your home!"

"I *have* the best of automation already," Cora stated firmly. What would these people think if they knew she'd been the one to name the Electro-Flex?

A laugh bubbled up inside her, accompanied by a nervous fluttering in her belly. Today was the day she finally got to put a face to Mr. Adam Levett.

"Coffee or tea?"

Cora jumped. That voice sounded familiar. When her eyes tracked to find the speaker, she jumped again. The handsome stranger from last night stood a mere ten paces away, looking exceedingly dapper in a navy blue suit, with no hat to conceal his unruly locks. Not seeming to have noticed her, he began walking backward. "Or both?" he asked, speaking to someone across the booth.

Cora darted to one side to avoid bumping into him for the second time in less than twenty-four hours. Perhaps that collision had been his fault, if he made a habit of walking without looking.

"Don't care," someone else called. "Just need something to kill the headache I'm getting from listening to that recording all day."

"Welcome to AutomaTech," Handsome Stranger imitated the mechanical voice as it began to play again. Laughing, he walked backward right past Cora, then spun and bounded away, presumably to fetch the requested beverages.

Oh, dear. This was an interesting complication. Did Handsome Stranger work here in the Palace of Electricity?

Perhaps even for AutomaTech? Maybe Levett knew him. Cora could ask him to introduce them properly.

Unless he counseled her to accept Benedict's courtship. That did seem the most logical course of action. If only she weren't woefully unattracted to him. He'd kissed her before, and it had been nothing but... wet.

Cora walked a quick lap around the area, until she spied a familiar device standing unused and unremarked upon by the people passing through. The Electro-Flex!

A young-ish man stood nearby. His blond hair was cut quite short, and he sported a tidy moustache that curled up at the ends. Handsome, she supposed, but not in a way that intrigued her. Could this possibly be Mr. Levett? This man couldn't be more than thirty. Cora had always imagined Levett as older. Bookish. Bespectacled. With wisps of gray hair or perhaps a bald spot. Someone with enough years to have amassed the vast amount of knowledge he possessed. And this man was too tidy. His narrow four-in-hand necktie was immaculate, his trousers creased to perfection. Cora had a difficult time imagining Levett investing so much of his time on clothing.

"Er, I'm looking for a Mr. Levett?" she asked. If this man was her friend, she feared she'd misread him entirely.

The man grinned at her. "You just missed him." His gaze raked over her. "He'll be disappointed to have missed a call from a pretty woman."

Cora blushed. Oh, no. Was this going to be like Benedict? Why were all the men interested in her not the ones she had any interest in? Fortunately, her inadequate flirting skills were likely to scare him off.

"Are you expecting Mr. Levett back sometime soon?" she asked, trying to keep her composure.

"You'd like to wait? No, he shouldn't be long. Although you never know with Levett. Sometimes he gets an idea and wanders off to go work on it."

That sounded like the Levett Cora knew. "I'd be happy to wait." She eyed the Electro-Flex. Why not use it while she passed the time? Her own device was back home, and it would do her good to give her muscles the extra work on the days she wasn't shooting. "May I?" she asked, reaching to lift the Electro-Flex down from its display stand.

"Oh! Certainly," the-man-who-was-not-Mr.-Levett replied, though his eyes had grown unusually round. "Uh, I can show you how it—"

He gaped at Cora's swift movements as she adjusted the device to the exact fit and sensitivity suited to an athlete prepping for the Olympic Games. She knew this machine better than anyone, possibly including Levett himself.

"Thank you," she said with a smile. "I believe I can manage."

· · · ❈ · · ·

What on earth had happened while he was gone?

Adam craned his neck to see the clock on the wall, since he couldn't check his pocket watch with his hands full of coffee. It had been precisely twelve minutes since he'd left and somehow the exhibit had transformed into a sensation in his absence.

"Welcome to AutomaTech," the automated voice recited, though the words were nearly drowned out by the buzz of the crowd.

Adam squirmed his way toward his display, rising up on tiptoe to see over the heads of the excited people in front of him. The coffee sloshed in his hands, splattering him with hot droplets. He stifled a curse caused less by the pain than by the sight in front of him.

There at the front of the crowd stood the woman from last night, her left sleeve pushed up past her elbow, and the Electro-Flex wrapped around her forearm. She pumped her arm up and down in rhythm with the movements of the device, in a technique that made perfect sense and left Adam wondering why he'd never thought of it before.

"As you can see," she explained, "the Electro-Flex uses a combination of electrical impulses and mechanical movement to stretch and strengthen my muscles. During rehabilitation after an injury, I began on the lowest setting, as any beginner would. The Electro-Flex did all the work for me. As I improved and increased the intensity of the workout, I began to move with the machine. Now, as you see, the machine and my own body work together in harmony, helping to keep me in top condition for my upcoming competition."

Damnation. The lovely young lady he'd acted a fool in front of was Miss Cora Maxwell after all. And she was more than he'd imagined. Prettier—though that hardly mattered, as he'd fallen in love with her before he'd had the slightest inkling what she looked like. But also smart, poised, well-spoken. Full of energy and life. Adam didn't fear speaking to a crowd, but he didn't excel at it, either. Cora practically glowed. She had something to say and a captive audience to say it to. How amazing must she be when she competed? The thought of watching her shoot for Olympic glory made him almost giddy.

Fuck.

No, no, no. He was supposed to be a friend to her, not fall even more in love with her than before.

"Coffee. Thank God."

Adam flinched when Doyle snatched a cup from his hand, once again avoiding a spill by the narrowest of margins.

"Do you know this girl?" Doyle asked. "She came looking for you."

"Miss Cora Maxwell." Adam surprised himself with the calm reply. "She's an archer. Here to compete in the Olympic Games."

Doyle leaned in and whispered, "How in the hell do *you* know anyone competing in the Games? Have you ever even entered a gymnasium?"

"I told you my Electro-Flex was endorsed by top athletes."

"Heh." Doyle took a swig of his coffee. "Thought that

was just marketing nonsense. To be honest, I wasn't sure the damned thing even worked."

"Would you stop swearing?" Adam hissed. "There are ladies watching. I don't want to be blamed if the company receives complaints."

"Why not? Thought you wanted to go into business for yourself."

"I do. But I need a good reputation for that."

"Electro-Flex," Doyle replied in a mock serious voice. "Best goddamned machine to get you off your lazy ass."

Adam struggled against the powerful urge to dump his coffee all over his friend's pristine suit. Instead, he took a fortifying sip of the strong brew and inched closer to Cora. She had rolled up her other sleeve and was now transferring the device to her right arm.

"The versatility of the design shows Mr. Levett's true brilliance," she said.

Adam choked on his coffee. Brilliant? She thought he was brilliant? This was not helping.

"The Electro-Flex is so easily adjustable that it can be used by persons large and small for all four limbs," Cora continued. It took her only seconds to strap the device in place and begin the exercises using her right arm. "I understand Mr. Levett has a design in development that will wrap around the torso to work the muscles of the back, shoulders, and abdominals."

Cora hadn't rolled down her left sleeve. Long scars from her injury and surgery stood out against her tanned skin. She had lovely forearms. Finely shaped and well-muscled from her athletic training.

Adam gulped more of his coffee. It burned going down, but he didn't care. He needed the distraction. He was out of his mind, to be contemplating the attractiveness of a woman's forearms.

Cora finished her demonstration for the enraptured crowd,

then returned the Electro-Flex to its display stand before rolling down and buttoning her sleeves.

What did she wear when she competed? A modest dress like the pale blue one she wore today? More likely something short-sleeved. Maybe short enough to bare her biceps as well. Adam wanted to see that. She probably had exceptionally well-formed biceps.

Or maybe she adopted some of the more daring trends of short skirts and corsets worn on the outside. He'd like to see that, too. Honestly, he'd like to see her in anything at all. Or nothing.

Adam looked down into his cup of coffee. It was nearly empty, and it had only made him jittery.

"Thank you for listening," Cora said to the buzzing audience. "I'm afraid I can't answer any questions about price or purchasing, as I'm only a consumer, not a salesperson. I'm sure there are others here who can provide you with that information. But I heartily offer my recommendation of Mr. Levett's device both for athletes and those recuperating from injury."

She kept mentioning him by name. She'd put him in the spotlight, right alongside his invention. Did she have any idea how much he appreciated that? He owed her.

"And if you will be here at the Exposition on September the nineteenth through twenty-first," he called out, "make certain to visit the athletic field to watch Miss Maxwell shoot in the Olympic archery competition. She will participate in two individual events and a team event, and she is sure to make our country proud."

Cora's head whipped around to stare at him. Their gazes locked. Her lips parted in surprise, then closed again as understanding dawned in her emerald eyes.

"Levett?" she asked.

Adam nodded. "Nice to meet you in person, Miss Maxwell."

3

Excerpt of a letter from Miss Cora Maxwell to Mr. Adam Levett, dated April 10, 1904

I hope I do not sound too presumptuous, but I feel we have become friends, and that you give sound advice. My training is being regularly interrupted by courtship. Mr. Howard is nice, I suppose, but I'd rather he not come by while I'm shooting. Should I tell him to go away? I'm not good with this sort of thing.

LEVETT WAS HER Handsome Stranger.

Cora tried to slow her agitated breathing and relax herself the way she did when preparing to shoot. Without the bow in her hand and a target to aim at, her body didn't respond as well to the routine. Her heart continued to beat wildly, and she struggled not to stare.

Levett was her Handsome Stranger.

Part of her mind continued to insist this was impossible. True, he was bespectacled, and slightly rumpled in the absent-minded way she'd expected. The top button of his vest was undone, his collar unstarched, and his necktie looser than strictly proper. But he was *young*. Her own age, or perhaps a bit older. Mid-twenties at most. And possessed of a smile that made her knees wobble.

This was bad.

Don't crush on Levett. Don't crush on Levett.

He was a friend. Her dearest friend. As much as she loved her girls back home, Levett was the one who listened best. Cora could tell he read every word of her letters. He responded promptly, thoughtfully, honestly. She could express her most outlandish opinions or deepest desires and know he wouldn't laugh or sigh. Well, probably. No laughter or sighing came across in his correspondence, at any rate.

Cora cherished their relationship, and if she messed it up because her ridiculous body found him delightful to look upon, she'd never forgive herself.

"Do you really shoot?" asked a girl of nine or ten, thankfully drawing Cora's attention away from Levett's mesmerizing hazel eyes. "With a real bow and arrow?"

"I do," Cora replied. "I started when I was six years old, but anyone of any age can learn."

The girl stared at her in awe. "I want to be in the Olympic Games when I grow up. I like to swim, but Daddy says girls don't swim in the Olympic Games."

Cora's jaw set. "Someday they will," she vowed. "Keep practicing."

The girl nodded gravely. Cora watched her walk off with her family, head held high.

I am a role model for these girls. A hero.

Cora shivered a little. Her. Awkward, doesn't-know-what-she's-doing Cora Maxwell. A hero. Wild.

She did know how to shoot, though, and still could, thanks to Levett and his remarkable machine. Cora would show the world what a woman could accomplish.

Levett had made his way to her side through the dwindling

crowd, and now stepped in front of her, eyes shining, his killer smile spreading ear-to-ear.

"Cora, I've had the most fantastic idea!" His brows knit together. "Oh. Er... pardon. I suppose I ought to call you Miss Maxwell?" He shrugged and his smile returned. "We should collaborate. Design sport and fitness products targeted specifically at women. It's an untapped market. People don't realize how many women enjoy athletic pursuits. We could begin a business and you could promote sport for ladies and girls at the same time!"

He bounced in place, unable to contain his restless enthusiasm. Cora had known him to be a man of great intellectual exuberance, but this physically energetic side of him surprised her. No wonder he bumped into people. He probably ran everywhere he went.

"I don't know sports well enough to know what sorts of machines might be helpful for playing or training or anything else tangentially related. But you do! You can give me ideas, test out my designs, help me market them. We'll be a sensation. Levett-Maxwell Technologies. The premier ladies' sporting manufacturer."

"Well, there's the obvious," Cora replied, unable to stop herself from joining in with his fanciful imaginings. "Devices to throw a baseball or swing a tennis racket. Resistance machines like the Electro-Flex for conditioning and strength training. Small, wearable gadgets to track your speed. Is that possible? Oh, what about an archery target that can give you feedback on the speed and power of your arrows?"

For a second she thought Levett might twirl around in delight, but he managed to still his fidgety body. "See? We'll do wonders! Let me find my notebook and then we can go talk." He did spin around now, looking bewildered and squinting through his spectacles. "It's here somewhere."

"Oh." Cora scanned the AutomaTech booth, finding no obvious place where he might have stashed a notebook.

The crowd had dissipated, but the AutomaTech employees remained, eyeing her. The blond man with the perfect suit was still smiling, but another employee stood across the booth with his arms folded, scowling at her. She had caused quite a ruckus, hadn't she?

"We can talk another time, Mr. Levett," she said in a rush. "I never meant to drag you away from your work, only to introduce myself in person."

"It's no trouble," his muffled voice replied. He'd bent over to dig through a crate beneath the Electro-Flex. It looked to be stuffed with papers, tools, and bits of metal. "Doyle can handle things without me."

"Oh, absolutely," the blond man replied. "Don't mind at all sitting here on my duff while you're busy flirting."

Levett's head snapped up so quickly he nearly bashed it on his own machine. "I'm not flirting!"

Cora winced. She didn't mind that he wasn't interested in her in that way, but hearing it exclaimed so vehemently was a bit embarrassing. She forced a laugh. "Of course not. How ridiculous would that be? Besides, I'm sure Mr. Levett has a sweetheart back home."

Doyle eyed her with raised eyebrows. "Are we talking about the same Levett? The one who spends all day, every day either writing letters or building peculiar inventions?"

Levett rose to his feet, notebook in hand. "Well, right now I'm going to spend part of the day walking the fairgrounds and chatting with my friend." He glanced at the scowling man. "I'll take over your later shift, Rawley. No need to have three of us here at once."

Rawley only sniffed.

Levett shrugged. "Right. Please excuse us."

He offered Cora his arm, and she took it, the thrill of touching him warming her skin. Hopefully he'd interpret it as embarrassment rather than excitement.

"Good luck!" Doyle called after them. "No need to hurry

back on my account! Take care not to put Miss Maxwell to sleep with all your blathering on."

Cora leaned toward Levett to whisper. "Is he always like this?"

"Oh, yes. Perpetual tease. But I'd trust him with my life."

"Oh." She straightened up. "That's good, I suppose." They walked on for a time in silence, until she could no longer hear the automated AutomaTech voice chattering away. "I'm sorry. I'm bad at talking."

The sudden renewal of conversation startled Levett from whatever reverie he'd been in. "Are you? Your letters flow so effortlessly. And you had that crowd enraptured."

"Yes, but, this." Cora waved a hand between the two of them. "Regular people talking. It's hard."

He laughed. "Well, we don't have to talk like regular people. We can talk like extraordinary people with a grand business plan. Now, tell me about this speed-sensing archery target you want."

Two hours later, Levett had a notebook filled with wild ideas, and Cora's conversational anxiety had vanished. They talked over and around one another like the good friends they were, knowing almost instinctively when to listen or when an interruption was acceptable.

"You must come with me tomorrow to watch the last of the track and field events," she exclaimed, clutching his arm with both hands now, as if touching him were the most natural thing in the world. It wasn't, yet. Her body reacted every bit as feverishly as it had when they'd collided last night. But she was determined to get it under control.

"I won't know what's going on or who to cheer for," he admitted. "But I can try."

"It's called a 'race.' The men line up and then they run very fast. The one who crosses the finish line first is the winner."

"Ha, ha, ha. I'm not *that* dense, you know."

Cora grinned. "I know. But it's fun to tease you. I think I understand your friend Doyle."

Levett smiled back at her. It warmed her, that smile. He wasn't exactly what she'd expected, but he was definitely the man she'd come to know through their letters. Interesting, kind, good-natured.

"Speaking of Doyle, I ought to return to my work and relieve him of his duties for a bit. But I *will* attend some athletic events with you tomorrow. I'll call it research." He took hold of Cora's hand, and for a wild moment she was certain he would lift it to his lips and kiss it. Then he shifted and gave her a firm handshake. "It was a pleasure meeting you face-to-face, Miss Maxwell. Until tomorrow."

Cora nodded. "The same to you, Mr. Levett."

He dipped his head and started off into the crowd, his steps rapid and energetic. Cora watched until he vanished from sight, then turned toward the athletic grounds. Her own step was light, eager for tomorrow to arrive. She'd found her friend, the meeting hadn't been a disaster, and their time enjoying the Exposition and the Olympic Games had only just begun.

The problem of her romantic life and her physical attraction to Levett nagged at her, but she forced the thoughts aside. She'd take up her bow and do some shooting. That would put it all out of her mind.

4

Excerpt of a letter from Mr. Adam Levett to Miss Cora Maxwell, dated September 30, 1903

I have learned more about the world of archery in these brief months of our correspondence than in the whole of my life. Do you enjoy other sports? I admit to having little knowledge of any athletic pursuit.

Sept. 3

"IF SOME SORT OF SENSOR could be placed at the finish line, to be triggered when the runner crosses, we could eliminate possible human error in race timing," Adam mused aloud. He drummed his fingers on his thigh. "A single switch could start the timer and sound a horn to replace the starter's pistol. And of course, you would need an output clock to read the time. Multiple clocks, to account for all the athletes. Or maybe a single clock with multiple arms? I'll have to think about that."

Cora glanced at him from where she leaned against the rail of the stadium seats, watching the runners and officials taking their places for the final heat of the 100-meter sprint. The corners of her mouth hitched up in amusement.

"You might never watch a single sporting event for the

sport itself," she said, "but at this rate you'll make yourself the king of athletic technology."

"Not a terrible realm to rule over, as far as I can see. And should I need assistance with understanding the minutiae of some particular sport, I will have you to advise me, as my, uh… high councillor? Vice president?" *Queen?*

"Captain of the guard," Cora replied in a deep, militaristic voice.

Adam laughed. "Indeed. With your legendary bow skills." Damn, but it was easy to converse with this woman. She didn't mind at all when he ran his mouth about whatever new idea popped in his head. Instead she'd been encouraging him all day. A bit disconcerting, that.

"Ooh. Pay attention!" She reached without looking and placed a hand on his thigh.

Desire pounded through him, starting where her hand rested and blazing a path to the furthest reaches of each and every limb. Cora withdrew her hand the instant she realized the impropriety, but the ghost of her touch remained, burning through him, making his heart pound with forbidden longing.

"The closest lane to us," Cora said, gesturing with the hand that had just unbalanced Adam's entire world. "Watch him."

Adam leaned toward her, close enough to catch a whiff of a clean, outdoorsy scent. He didn't know enough about either flowers or ladies' scents to discern more.

"Why him?"

"That's Archie Hahn," she explained. "Best sprinter in the world. He's already won the 60-meter and 200-meter events. He'll win this one too, don't doubt it."

Adam detected nothing especially remarkable about the runner. Hahn wasn't very tall or imposing, though he did look fit, and when he took his stance at the starting line he did so with an expression of fierce determination and an aura of coiled energy ready to be unleashed.

The heat was over nearly as soon as it had begun, with

Hahn flying down the track past the spectators to easily outpace the remainder of the field. Cora hopped up and applauded as the official medalists and the winning time were announced. Eleven seconds. Adam didn't even want to think about how little ground he would have covered in the same amount of time. Perhaps when he worked on his timing mechanisms he could recruit real runners to test them so he wouldn't have to embarrass himself.

"That was amazing!" Cora exclaimed. "I'm so glad we were able to be here to see it."

Adam couldn't help but smile at her delight. She'd been right. He'd never have come to this event just to watch it for himself. But watching with her was fun. Even better than the research for his athletic technologies.

"What other events are scheduled before your archery?" He'd attend them all if she liked.

"Archery!" exclaimed a male voice from just behind Adam. "I knew I recognized you."

Adam and Cora turned together.

"George Thompson." The tall, mousey-haired man extended a hand toward Adam. "Potomac Archery Club."

Adam shook the man's hand, for lack of a better idea. "Adam Levett." When Mr. Thompson showed no inclination to shake Cora's hand as well, Adam added, "And this is Miss Cora Maxwell."

Thompson nodded to Cora. "Miss Maxwell. I gather you take an interest in my sport? I noticed you shooting yesterday."

Cora smiled, but her jaw was tight. "More than an interest, Mr. Thompson. I have been a competitive archer for a full decade. I am here to win Olympic gold."

"Oh?" Thompson chuckled. "You did shoot well from what I saw. That was at what? Thirty yards?" The condescension in his smug smile caused a surge of fury inside Adam.

The vehemence of the sudden emotion startled him. He

was debating what he ought to do about it when Cora stepped in to handle the situation on her own.

"I would certainly hope I shot well at thirty yards," she replied coolly, "since that was my warmup distance."

"Ah," Thompson replied, his haughty air not diminishing. "Well, if you'd ever like some coaching from a professional, I'll be around."

Punching him in the face sounded satisfying. Adam flexed his fingers, debating his ability to do so without injuring his hand. Perhaps knocking Thompson on his ass would be better. Preferably in a mud puddle. In front of a large crowd.

"I don't believe I have any need of your assistance, Mr. Thompson," Cora answered. Her smile was as feral as a wolf's. Delightful, when directed at an enemy. Adam looked forward to watching her rip Thompson to pieces. "But if you ever need a bit of competition during your practicing, let me know. I'm always ready to face down a new opponent."

Thompson raised a single eyebrow. "Is that a challenge, Miss Maxwell?"

Cora drew herself up to her full height, tipping her broad hat back to give him a clear look at the ferocity in her emerald gaze. "Yes. It is."

5

Excerpt of a letter from Miss Cora Maxwell to Mr. Adam Levett, dated October 2, 1903

I am certain the Electro-Flex will be beneficial for athletes of all sports. Strength, stamina, and flexibility are an asset in any athletic pursuit.

Sept. 4

Cora stormed through the Palace of Electricity and Machinery, looking neither left nor right as she plowed past vendors and exhibitors.

"Cleaning rats for home and—Hey! Watch it!"

She narrowly avoided crushing the small mechanical creature as it darted to gobble up the latest mess. Only days ago she'd arrived in St. Louis with eyes wide, eager to immerse herself in the excitement of the Exposition. This morning she couldn't bring herself to care.

Even after a full night's sleep, Mr. Thompson's disdain still rankled. Yes, she was one of only a handful of women competing in the Olympic Games, but it wasn't by chance.

She'd earned that place. Her local and regional victories had qualified her to shoot against anyone in the country.

And then this man—this fellow athlete—mocked her.

Cora had taken up her bow, set up seventy-five yards from the target, and shot until her arms ached and her legs were wobbly from walking to retrieve her arrows over and over and over. With every thwack of the arrow into the target, she'd imagined Thompson dressed in battle armor, staggering from an arrow that had struck a weak point, stunned he'd been conquered by a woman. She would defeat him. She'd defeated plenty of men in the course of her sporting career.

Today, though, after such an arduous practice, she would be stretching and resting. Using low settings on the Electro-Flex to soothe and rejuvenate her sore muscles. She wouldn't even have come today if it weren't for the Electro-Flex. Her mood remained grim and not a single marvel of the fair could pique her interest.

"Welcome to AutomaTech! The leader in affordable mail-order technology. Browse the AutomaTech catalog today and bring the best of automation into your home!"

The booth was unoccupied this morning, though someone had obviously turned on the electric lights and the recorded welcome message. Cora walked straight to the Electro-Flex, lifted it down and strapped it on. It felt good on low. Just enough to get her muscles moving without overworking. Fifteen minutes on each arm, and then she'd leave. Maybe go for a walk about town. Or head down to the docks and watch ships puff by along the Mississippi. She could sit in her hotel and read, but not for too long. She'd been anticipating spending most of her waking time exploring the Exposition or watching the Olympic events and hadn't brought much reading material.

"Just what do you think you're doing?" a voice boomed.

Cora whirled to discover a gray-haired man standing in the entrance to the AutomaTech area. A large mechanical dog stood beside him. A deep growling sound emanated from its open jaw.

"That is delicate and valuable technology," the man scolded. "Can't you read?" He jabbed a finger toward one of the many signs stating, *Do Not Touch!*

"Of course I can read," Cora shot back, too annoyed to bother with civility. "I'm Cora Maxwell, the athlete who endorsed and named the Electro-Flex."

"What? Don't be ridiculous. Women aren't athletes."

"I assure you, I am. I'm here to compete at the Olympic Games. I'm a friend of Mr. Levett and a long-time user of his machine. I did a live demonstration with this very machine the other day to great acclaim. Did you not hear of it?"

"Hogwash! Levett knows better..." The man shook his head. "Perhaps not. Boy can be a bit flighty at times. But Doyle would have been here, and he never—"

"Mr. Doyle witnessed the same event. He and Mr. Levett were happy to allow me to return to use the machine at any time. I assure you, everyone here at the exhibit was pleased with the demonstration and the interest it generated."

"A fine story," the man snarled. "Unfortunately, you've chosen the wrong man to tell it to. I am James Hampton, founder and president of AutomaTech, and I know my engineers better than you possibly could. They would not permit any unsupervised person to play with such sophisticated technology."

Play? The unmitigated arrogance of this man! Of all men! If anyone ever asked her again why she was unmarried or why she was so reluctant to accept Benedict's suit, *this* was going to be her answer. Men were jackasses.

Hampton held out a hand. "Hand over the machine, Miss Maxwell."

Cora made one last effort. "Mr. Hampton, I assure you, I am fully qualified to use and demonstrate this apparatus. I am an Olympic athlete who uses the Electro-Flex as a vital part of my training regimen. Mr. Levett and I have been in regular contact for over a year. He knows all about my use of the device, and I know all the details of his work on perfecting and marketing it. If you allow me a moment to show you—"

Hampton grabbed at her arm, catching one of the straps of the Electro Flex and tugging it loose even though the machine was still running.

"No, don't!"

She tried to spin away, but Hampton was strong, and faster than she expected. He began to yank and twist the adjustments on the Electro-Flex, trying to pry it off her. The machine groaned in protest.

"Stop! You're going to break it!"

One of the brass supports snapped, and the machine loosened around Cora's arm. Hampton pulled it off over her hand as it continued whirring, its usual purr now a strangled whine.

"What's going on?"

Levett. Oh, no. He'd be crushed. His machine ruined. His purpose here destroyed.

His jaw fell open when he spied his broken creation. Shock and horror filled his hazel eyes. "What happened to the Electro-Flex?"

"I found this woman engaged in unauthorized tampering with the product." Hampton plunked the Electro-Flex down on its pedestal, not even bothering to shut it down. The apparatus vibrated mournfully, broken brass supports waving where they dangled unnaturally.

Levett's gaze darted between Hampton and Cora. "Cor— Miss Maxwell knows every nuance of that machine," he replied, his voice rough with pain and disbelief. "And she *was* authorized."

"By you?" Hampton asked.

"Yes, by me. Who else?"

"The rules for this exhibition explicitly stated that the devices were to be operated only by certified AutomaTech employees. And for exactly this reason." He jerked a hand at the damaged machine. "See what has happened?"

"*You* did that," Cora retorted. She would not let this horrible man make her look bad in front of her friend. "You ripped it off me."

Hamption glared at her for a moment, then turned back to Levett. "You're fired. Gather your things and don't come back."

Cora clapped a hand to her mouth to cover her gasp. Dear God. What had she done?

6

Excerpt of a letter from Mr. Adam Levett to Miss Cora Maxwell, dated December 11, 1903

I do dream of someday starting my own business, but at the moment I am content working at AutomaTech. As long as I can tinker and create, I'm happy.

ADAM'S MIND HAD GONE NUMB. He couldn't seem to speak, or even think. His body moved of its own accord, pulling out the crate from beneath the Electro-Flex, and shoving aside his papers and notebooks to fit the broken machine inside.

What had just happened? This couldn't be reality. He must have misunderstood. And yet his hands kept moving, gathering up his things. Preparing for a departure that seemed impossible, yet inevitable.

Hampton watched him, silently, his hard mouth fixed in a scornful scowl. Did he expect some response? A plea? Stunned as Adam was, he didn't think he could form any coherent argument. He wouldn't have wanted to, regardless. He wasn't giving Hampton that satisfaction.

Adam hefted the crate in both arms and strode away, his

body still ahead of his stupefied mind. Past Hampton's big, ugly, useless pet dragon. Through the gates and by the equally useless guard dragons. On and on, away from the automated voice he hoped never to hear again in his life.

"Welcome to AutomaTech," he muttered. "Where you can go fuck yourself."

"I'm so sorry."

Adam cringed, whether from the sound of Cora's voice or the soft brush of her hand against his arm, he didn't know.

"I apologize for my inappropriate language," he said, shaking off the last of the fog. What was done was done. He'd move on. Sit down and think and decide his next steps.

"No, don't apologize," Cora replied. "I should apologize. Levett, I'm so sorry. I had no idea. If I'd had any inkling someone would respond that way I would have…" She shook her head. "I don't know. Taken the Electro-Flex somewhere else? Waited to use it until you were present? I don't know. But it wouldn't have been this."

Adam shrugged as best he could manage with his arms full of the crate. "It was going to happen sooner or later. Hampton's wanted me gone for ages. When I first proposed the design for the Electro-Flex, he scoffed at it. Said it wasn't marketable. So I built it on my own time and promoted it to doctors and medical technicians. It was only after your endorsement and the new name that Hampton relented and allowed it in his catalog. He still thought it wouldn't sell. But it has. I get a percentage of every sale. If Hampton had done things differently, that money would have gone to AutomaTech. Though I think that bothers him less than the fact I proved him wrong."

"I'm still sorry it ended like this. And in the middle of your time here. What will happen now? Will you be forced to leave?"

Adam froze. One of the ubiquitous cleaning rats scuttled past his feet. "I… hadn't thought of that yet. My hotel is paid by the company. I suppose they'll kick me out. But I'm not leaving town before your events. I want to watch you compete."

Cora's cheeks pinkened. "And I want you here cheering me on. But I would feel terrible if you had to pay for a new room. You can stay with me, if you need a place."

Adam's heart lurched. A fraction of a second later, a weight dropped in his gut. If ever he'd needed a reminder that she didn't consider him in a romantic light, this was it. The offer to share her accommodations had been effortless, without hesitation. As if the proposition weren't entirely scandalous. Exactly the sort of offer she would have made for a female friend.

"That is very kind of you, Miss Maxwell," he replied. Could she hear the slight waver in his voice? Could she sense the desire pounding through him? How much he wanted to shout, *Yes, yes! Let me into your room. Into your life. Into your heart.* "But it would be wholly inappropriate."

"Oh." She frowned a moment, but he couldn't guess what she might be thinking. "I don't see how that matters. It's a busy hotel during an exceptionally busy time. No one knows us. The chances of anyone even noticing are miniscule."

"The hotel staff would notice, though, when they came to clean. But the point is moot. Doyle has a room just across the hall from me. He'll let me stay with him."

"Ah. That's the most sensible plan, then."

"Yes." Adam needed sensible. He needed whatever it took to prevent himself fantasizing that Cora might feel the same sort of attraction to him that he felt for her.

Adam stepped out the doors of the Palace of Electricity and Machinery for what he intended to be the last time, and started on the path that would take him around the southern end of the Grand Basin. On all sides fairgoers smiled and pointed, enjoying their sightseeing. He was one of them now, he supposed. A man here on his own time. Before, he'd always been apart from the crowd. Focused on his work. Walking the paths without stopping to look.

What would happen now that he was at his leisure? At the moment, he couldn't imagine being as carefree as these people looked.

"Where are we headed?" Cora asked. "Do you need to catch a train or a steam cab to your hotel?"

"I'm staying at the Inside Inn," Adam answered, using the familiar name for the massive hotel built within the Exposition grounds. "It's less than a mile. I just walk."

"Good exercise. And you walk quickly."

He slowed. "Am I too fast for you? My legs are much longer than yours."

Cora only laughed. "I'm an athlete. I can jog to keep up if I need to."

Adam grinned at her and resumed his usual pace. "Will it help with your archery? Better shooting through general fitness?"

"Yes. Anything that strengthens my body is helpful." Her gaze drifted away from him. "Will you be able to fix the Electro-Flex?"

His smile vanished. "No. Not with the tools I have on hand. I'm so sorry. I know you wanted to use it for your training."

Cora lifted one shoulder, then let it drop. "I brought a long, stretchy rubber hose with me for resistance exercises. It won't be as good as the machine, but it's lightweight and portable, which is why I chose it over bringing my personal Electro-Flex. Back to my original plan, that's all."

Adam nodded, trying to appear more optimistic than he felt. His inability to fix the machine only compounded his dejection. He'd lost his job, but she'd suffered too. Not merely from the loss of the Electro-Flex, but from her guilt over her role in the debacle.

"What about you?" she asked, because of course her greatest concern was for him. "What will you do?"

"What I always wanted to do. Go into business for myself. We'll start our new company making athletic machines. Fitness Tech."

Cora pulled a face. "You choose the worst names. I'll think up a better one. But what will you do *now*? You said you wanted to stay to watch me compete. Will you spend your days exploring the fair, or have you seen it all already?"

"I've hardly given it a thought outside of work. But I know my way around, so I suppose I should take advantage of that."

Cora's fingers brushed his arm again, briefly. "We could explore together."

The same sharp burst of desire that had hit when she'd offered to share her hotel room surged through him.

"I would like that very much."

A new grin began to tug at the corners of Adam's mouth. Maybe his sudden unemployment was a blessing. He had two weeks free now, to fill himself with the joy of her friendship. He could spend all day, every day with her. Take whatever he could get of her. Seeing her in person was already better than her letters ever had been. Wishing for more was futile, but he'd be damned if he didn't wring every last drop of pleasure from what he had.

7

Excerpt of a letter from Mr. Adam Levett to Miss Cora Maxwell, dated August 24, 1903

Congratulations, Miss Maxwell! I knew you would do well at your tournament. I can tell already you have the heart of a champion.

Sept. 5

*A*DAM HELD HIS BREATH as Cora drew back the string of her bow. Her sleeveless dress afforded him a view of the flexing of her arm muscles. Her grip was strong, steady, her expression composed. She loosed the arrow, and Adam's breath rushed out in time with the flying projectile. The tip embedded itself directly in the center of the bullseye.

"You really are good," he marveled. "I mean, I knew you were, from everything you wrote about your competitions, but seeing it in person... You made that look so easy."

Cora laughed. "I'm only warming up. When Thompson arrives, we'll be shooting from twice this distance." Her expression hardened. "*If* he ever arrives."

"He'll show. He'd look cowardly to refuse the challenge.

And I'm sure he thinks he can wander up at the last moment and easily 'put you in your place.'"

Cora scowled. "Men." She released another arrow, and it slammed into the target with such force that Adam flinched.

"Er, yes."

Adam found himself a shady spot to lounge against a tree, arms crossed over his chest as he watched her complete her warmups. Her clothing had been chosen with care. The lack of sleeves gave her complete freedom of movement and prevented anything catching on her forearm guard or her bow. Her skirt was lightweight and loose enough not to interfere with her stance. She could have worn trousers or a shorter skirt, but he suspected that choice was deliberate too. The dark brown of her corset stood out against the white of the dress. Cora didn't want to simply win. She wanted to show she could win while wearing a corset and a floor-length skirt.

"Miss Maxwell."

Adam and Cora turned together at the sound of Thompson's smarmy voice. He strode toward them, bow in hand and a quiver of arrows slung over his shoulder. Adam moved to stand at Cora's side, ready to back her up should she need it.

"You look prepared for our friendly match," Thompson said, smirking.

Adam leaned in to whisper in Cora's ear. "Shall I explain the meaning of 'friend' to him? He seems to misunderstand it."

Her mouth twitched. "I am fully prepared, Mr. Thompson," she replied. Her wolfish smile was back. Adam adored it. It was terrifying, and perhaps a little arousing. Didn't Thompson see how ferocious this woman was? Especially since she held a deadly weapon in her hand.

Cora collected her arrows and stashed them in her quiver. "Shall we pace off, Mr. Thompson? I think sixty yards shall do."

"Sixty?" he echoed. "A bit far for a lady, don't you think?"

"No. Five rounds of six? Or do you prefer more?"

"Five rounds is plenty." Thompson's condescending expression hadn't altered a bit. "No sense in dragging this out longer than necessary."

Adam trailed behind as Cora paced off the distance. She took a moment to study her path to the target, then scratched a mark in the ground with the heel of her boot.

"There." She gestured at Thompson. "Feel free to shoot first."

He shrugged. "If you prefer." He stepped up to the line and fired off six arrows in rapid succession. Adam didn't know much about archery, but the results didn't impress him. The arrows were all over the target, rather than clustered in the center as Cora's warmup shots had been. From Thompson's casual attitude, Adam guessed he thought he could beat Cora without much effort.

Cora and Thompson tallied the points together as Thompson retrieved his arrows. The scoring system was straightforward: a single point for the outermost white ring, two for the next, and so on, up to ten points for the center yellow circle. Adam appreciated the mathematical simplicity of it. Cora took up her place at the line. Her stance was as relaxed as when she'd been warming up, her body still but not strained. Her expression, however, was one of intense concentration. Those green eyes of hers stared down the target. Adam caught himself holding his breath again. At this moment, did she even know he was here, watching? He wouldn't have wagered on it.

The arrow flew, smacking into the red portion of the target. She nocked another and released it, with the same result. By the time she finished the round, five of her six arrows were within the red and yellow circles. Three points better than Thompson.

Thompson's expression hardened, and when he took aim to begin round two, his posture more closely resembled Cora's. Deliberate. Determined. He'd stopped underestimating her.

He performed better in the second round, collected his

arrows, then propped himself against a tree. As he watched Cora, he pulled a sandwich from a pocket and took a single bite, chewing slowly. His expression was no longer mocking, but calculated. He picked off a bit of bread and tossed it at a nearby bird.

Cora erred on one of her shots in the second round and ceded a point to Thompson, but retained her lead. When he eyed her with clear distaste, she smiled back, as cool as ever.

The contest continued, rising in intensity with every shot. Adam's gaze darted repeatedly toward the athletic field. Cora had asked permission to set up for practice here alongside it, but this had gone far beyond casual shooting already, and Adam suspected the Olympic officials wouldn't like impromptu games occurring during their event. As much as he wanted to see her beat Thompson, he wanted her to stay out of trouble more.

Point by point Cora increased her lead, edging out Thompson in both the third and fourth rounds. With every arrow she shot, his jaw tightened, and more wrinkles appeared on his brow. He abandoned any attempt to eat his sandwich in favor of hurling angry crumbs on the ground and watching birds fight for them.

Adam paced back and forth, wearing a trampled path in the sod. Why did people like sport? When you actually cared who won, it was excruciating.

Cora's form remained perfect, her shots true. She nocked her final arrow, staring down the target. Adam couldn't see exactly where her shots had hit from this distance, but he could tell enough to approximate her current points. All she needed was to hit the blue to claim victory.

The instant before she released her arrow, Thompson chucked his final piece of bread—this time directly at Cora's feet. Half a dozen birds darted after it, tangling in her skirts and throwing her off-balance. Her shot went wide, sticking into the outermost white ring.

She whirled around, cheeks furiously red, eyes shimmering with rage.

"Excellent contest," Thompson said cooly, his former smirk returning.

The only time Adam recalled wanting to do violence to a person this badly was when he'd been twelve and a boy at school had deliberately stomped on his spectacles. His fingers clenched into tight fists and he stalked toward Thompson.

"You goddamned bastard," Adam swore. He'd apologize to Cora later. Thompson didn't deserve civilized language.

Thompson only laughed. "Aww. Disappointed your sweetheart didn't defeat me? You do realize it's supposed to be the *man* who shows off his feats of skill to the ladies, don't you?"

Adam jabbed a finger in Thompson's direction. "You're a cheat. A cheat, a woman-hater, and a damned coward."

Hatred blazed in Thompson's eyes. He raised a fist. Like Cora, his arms were well-muscled from years of practice with the bow. He could probably knock Adam out cold with a single punch.

"You want to say that again, four-eyes?"

"You want me to take it back?" Adam snarled. "Then give Miss Maxwell another shot. A *fair* shot."

"She lost. Thirty shots. We're done here."

Adam hadn't expected a different response, but now at least he could say he'd given the man a chance to repent. He stared directly into Thompson's face.

"You. Are. A. Coward."

Thompson's fist flew, but Adam ducked the blow and darted a few steps away. He wasn't athletic, but he was fast. And he'd dodged bullies before.

"Enough!"

Both men spun toward Cora. Still flushed with righteous anger, she held a bow in both hands, ready to smash it over her knee. Thompson's bow, that he'd set down while luring birds to do his dirty work.

"If you lay a finger on Mr. Levett," Cora threatened, "I will smash this into pieces and use it for firewood. Then we'll see how well you shoot."

Thompson dropped his fist, glaring back and forth between Adam and Cora. "You'll be sorry. Both of you."

Cora gestured with the bow. "Get lost." Only after Thompson retrieved his quiver and took a few steps away did she toss the bow to him.

He brandished it like a sword. "You'll be sorry," he repeated and stormed away.

Adam laid a hand on Cora's shoulder, only for a moment, but long enough to rekindle the urge to wrap his arms around her and kiss her senseless.

"Wait right here." He hoped she'd mistake the edge in his voice for lingering anger.

Keeping an eye on Thompson's retreating back, Adam jogged to the target, counted up Cora's points and pulled out the misfired arrow.

"Let's see how you do with a real shot," he said, when he handed it over to her. "Hit even the outer blue ring and you win."

Cora gave Adam a smile that nearly made his knees buckle. "Just you watch."

She took a long, slow breath, then lifted the bow, nocked her arrow, and aimed. Adam didn't even look at the target as she let the arrow fly. But, oh, did he watch. Her body was poised. Strong. Skilled. And her face. God, her face was glorious. Her eyes were fixed in concentration, her mouth a tight line. So focused, so resolute. The face of a champion.

The thwack behind him told him when the arrow hit the target. The smile that curved on Cora's lips told him all the rest.

"Bullseye," he said.

She grinned now, picking up her quiver and slinging it over her shoulder. "Damn right it was."

8

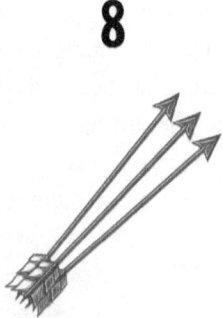

Excerpt of a letter from Miss Cora Maxwell to Mr. Adam Levett, dated March 12, 1904

Have you ever worked with audio technology? I spotted a new autogramophone in the latest AutomaTech catalog and it made me think of you. I'm sure you could think up many interesting things to do with sound recording and playback technologies. What I really want is a tiny gramophone that I can carry in my pocket or attach to a belt so I can play music wherever I go. I'm a huge fan of music. It can be fun, relaxing, exciting, melancholy, and so much more. I'm not very picky about my music, either. I love marching bands, orchestral suites, choral performances, ragtime, and others I can't even think of at the moment. My collection of gramophone discs is rather large, as you can imagine. What about you? What are your favorite sorts of music? Do you play any instruments?

Sept. 5, evening

HE REMEMBERED. Not some vague memory that she liked music, either. Levett had rattled off every detail of what Cora had written, as if he'd read her letter until he memorized it.

She opened up her mouth to reply, but only a few garbled syllables came out.

"What was that?" Levett stepped closer, his arm brushing hers. "It's awfully loud and chaotic here." All around them people chattered, vendors hawked their wares, and musicians struck up lively tunes. The sun had set hours before, but here on the Pike, the fair was still in full swing.

"I'm just impressed you remembered all my musical preferences," Cora managed to finally say.

Levett shrugged. "Well, you professed to like all music, so it's not difficult to remember." He grinned at her from behind his spectacles. The light from the arc lamps up and down the mile-long entertainment venue sparkled in his hazel eyes. "I regret that I haven't been able to devise a way to make a gramophone small enough to fit in a pocket for you. I'm sure it's possible, but I haven't had time to devote to the project." He laughed. "I guess now I've got nothing but time, so maybe I'll get back to it."

Cora nodded, unable to adopt the same carefree attitude he'd taken to his unemployment. She ought never to have permitted him to buy her that hotdog, but she'd never had one before, and he'd insisted she needed to try it. If he offered to purchase any more food during this outing, she'd remember to refuse.

Or at least remember to try. Denying Levett was difficult when he was so dratted *nice*. Cora loved the way he'd defended her after Thompson had disrupted her final shot. Not with fists, but with words. He'd been outraged on her behalf and unafraid to call out the unsportsmanlike behavior. He was every bit as supportive as he'd seemed from his letters. Thoughtful, a good listener, and genuinely interested in what she had to say. Combined with his gorgeous smile and handsome features, he made a very dangerous package.

Cora stepped just far enough away that they wouldn't bump as they walked. Ridiculous as it was, every accidental touch sent fire racing through her body. Not what she needed. What she did need was to enjoy this pleasant time with a friend and put the rest of the day behind her.

A dancer in a dress with several brightly colored layers swirled past, moving in time to the rhythmic strums of a stringed instrument. A young musician followed behind her, his fingers never faltering even as he meandered through the crowd. Men and women walking the streets clapped, and some tossed coins that the dancer caught in a small purse.

"Do you know what country they're from?" Cora asked Levett. So many things here were new to her. So much she didn't know. Which, she supposed, was the stated purpose of a World's Fair. To expose people to things they might never otherwise see.

"Spain," Levett replied. "Though I couldn't say which area of that nation they hail from. I do like the music."

"So do I. I wish I could hear music from every country represented here at the fair, though I'm certain that's nearly impossible. Still, I would like to know. We're all so different, yet all so much the same. We all have music, art, dance, stories. Do you think these are the things that make us human?"

"Uh…" Levett paused and turned to gaze into her eyes. "That's a very heavy question. And a good observation. We do share many fundamental things with all people. Why do we focus on what's different rather than what's the same?"

"I don't know. But it's nice to have someone to discuss such things with." *Someone who doesn't think I'm odd or that women shouldn't bother themselves with scientific and philosophical subjects.*

"I absolutely agree."

Levett grinned, making Cora warm all over, even without touching him. She took a slow breath similar to the ones she used while calming herself during archery. Clearly she had no recourse but to ignore her body's lustfulness. It couldn't be too hard. She'd been doing it for years. It was odd, though, to be so attracted to a friend. One she intended to spend the entirety of the next two weeks with.

Well. Not kissing him would be a good exercise in self-discipline. Important for an athlete.

Cora forced herself to resume walking, and was rewarded with a distraction not far ahead.

"Oh!" She broke into a jog. "Look at that water chute ride!" Cora pointed at the wide ramp, several hundred feet long, spilling down into a rectangular pool. Boxy, flat-bottomed boats rose up a pair of conveyor belts to the top, where delighted passengers boarded for the thrilling plunge. "We must try that tomorrow! And the roller coaster behind it, running all up and down those hills!"

The riders in the boat and train cars looked to be packed in tightly. Sitting so close with Levett would certainly test her ability to not think about kissing him. But it would be worth it.

"And the Observation Wheel," Levett added, jogging a few steps to catch up with her. "I've been wanting to ride that since I arrived here."

Cora slowed and looked at him. "Why haven't you? Too busy working?"

"I was waiting for you." Was he blushing? Or was that an illusion caused by these odd electric lights?

"Oh. Thank you. I'm very much looking forward to it."

"As am I." Adam paused to check the time. "Yikes. It's past ten. I'm sorry. I should have been paying closer attention. And you catch your train all the way down past the other end of the Pike, don't you? We'll have to walk the whole mile back."

Cora spun around. "No trouble. The Pike is open until eleven. We have plenty of time. But please don't feel you have to walk me all the way to the train. You'd have another mile after that to walk back to your hotel. But if you leave from this end you can just take a diagonal path and save a great deal of walking."

Levett offered her his arm. "I'd rather have the honor of

seeing my lovely friend safely on her way before I head for home."

Lovely friend. Cora mulled over his words as they trekked the mile to the main entrance and her transportation. Was that compliment referring to their friendship? Or did he actually mean she was lovely? In an "I am attracted to you" sense? Cora tried to wrap her head around the possible implications. What would she do if he possessed feelings similar to her own? They were friends and she didn't want to ruin that. She would never wish to make him feel awkward or uncomfortable in any way.

But if they both wanted to kiss…

"You've grown quiet," Levett observed. "Is it the late hour? Or have you simply had your fill of all this commotion? It does make rather the stark contrast to the quiet intensity of your archery."

"I don't mind the noise. I was lost in thought, is all."

He nodded. "I get like that too. Often."

Cora chuckled. "Yes. I'd noticed. You seem very full of ideas."

"Too full, sometimes."

A lull fell over the conversation again. Many others were now abandoning the fair for cabs and trains and the promise of a bed for the night. They'd be back bright and early tomorrow, ready to explore some new corner of the massive fairground.

Cora and Levett stopped at the main gates, facing one another to say their goodbyes. "Goodnight, Mr. Levett. I'll leave you to return to your hotel, now. What time shall we meet in the morning?"

"Nine a.m.? Or is that too early?"

"Nine a.m. is fine. Right here?"

"Yes." He took a step toward her. Cora's breath caught in her throat. This was inappropriately close, yet it wasn't close enough. Not close enough to feel his body. Not close enough to kiss him. "Cora," he murmured.

She took her own step forward, covering almost all the

remaining space. Levett stared down at her, his gaze lingering on her mouth. He *did* feel it too. This heat, this energy between them flowed from both sides, colliding in the middle to create a radiant spark, like the arc lights that shone down upon them.

She wanted to taste that spark. She wanted to feel that electricity racing through her body.

"Thank you for a beautiful day," he whispered. "You astounded me with your athletic skills and took me on a fun, if noisy, after-dinner jaunt. I may run back to my hotel just to make tomorrow come all the sooner."

"You're welcome." Cora rose on her tiptoes, giving him every opportunity to kiss her. "It was lovely for me, also."

His fingers brushed hers, and she jolted at the sudden contact. Levett sprang backward, ending any opportunity for a kiss.

"G-goodnight, Miss Maxwell." He made an awkward bow. "I'll see you in the morning."

"Goodnight." Cora turned away slowly, a bit stunned by what had almost happened. She wasn't sure whether they'd had a lucky escape or a missed opportunity. She'd probably wonder about it all night, and suspected Levett might be doing the same.

One short train ride later, she tucked herself into bed, tracing her lips with a finger, imagining what it would feel like when he pressed his mouth to hers.

Not if. She was certain of that much. *When.*

9

Excerpt of a letter from Mr. Adam Levett to Miss Cora Maxwell, dated Aug. 13, 1903

I'm afraid I'm not remotely athletic, myself. Twice as a boy I fell and injured myself trying to climb a telegraph pole. (Which I was climbing in order to investigate the technology. I couldn't just climb trees like a normal person.) And while my parents made me learn to swim well enough not to drown, I am quite certain my technique resembles that of an angry cat.

Sept. 6

$\mathcal{S}$ADLY, CORA WAS NOT afraid of heights. The woman sitting directly in front of Adam clung to the man beside her, giggling in feigned or exaggerated fright as the boat prepared for the 350 foot drop down the water chute.

"Of course I'll keep you safe, darling," the man replied, placing an arm around her shoulders.

Jealousy was not an attractive emotion, but at the moment Adam was failing any attempt at self-betterment. He wanted what that other couple had. He wanted to snuggle close to Cora and protect her. Or have her protect him. Both scenarios were equally acceptable. Unfortunately, he wasn't afraid of heights, either, and pretending he was to get her to touch him would be reprehensible.

He'd spent the entire walk back to his hotel last night wishing he'd kissed her, then berating himself for thinking any such thing. He'd no right. She was seeing someone back home. Maybe. All her mentions of the situation in her letters had sounded conflicted. Perhaps even confused. Regardless, Adam had no business interfering. No matter how enchanting she'd looked beneath the glow of electric lights.

The boat rocked forward, and the woman in front of him squealed in the delighted, frightened way of so many thrill ride passengers.

"Here we go!" Cora exclaimed. Her hand settled atop Adam's, but before he could even contemplate what that might mean, the barge was hurtling down the chute. Seconds later, it plunged into the water, sending a spray of droplets across its passengers—enough to feel refreshing without leaving the riders damp. Several people whooped. One man clapped.

Cora's fingers squeezed Adam's. "That was brilliant! Shall we go again, or—" A sudden impact with the bottom of the boat set the craft rocking. Several passengers yelped. "What was that?"

This time Adam heard the thud, as whatever it was beneath the water slammed into their small barge once again. The boat listed to one side, sending Adam sliding into Cora. A woman screamed.

"Help!" cried the man in front of Cora, his arm still wrapped around his lady friend.

A third time, the unseen object struck the boat, tipping it at least forty-five degrees past horizontal. Adam grabbed for the back of the seat, but his hands couldn't find a grip. His fingers slipped across the wet wood and he toppled into the pool, the other passengers tumbling and shouting around him.

The water was cold and murky, and for a few terrifying

seconds Adam wasn't certain which way was up. He flailed his arms and legs, trying to orient himself. How deep was the water? Where was Cora?

Oh, God, oh God. They were going to drown and he'd never told her how he felt. He'd never kissed her.

His feet hit solid ground. One arm broke the surface. A moment later, he'd righted himself, gulping in the fresh air. The water came only to mid-chest. Cora stood beside him, her head fully above the surface. All around them, the other passengers helped one another stand and pushed damp hats and hair back from their faces.

"What the devil was that?" one man swore.

"There!" A woman pointed at a scaled metal tail, diving below the surface. "One of those dragon creatures!"

Up on the pavement, a crowd of sightseers had gathered, chattering and staring at the sodden group. Fair workers at the water chute docks rushed around, moving people out of the way and racing to shut down the ride.

"Someone help us!" called the man who'd been seated in front of Cora. Both he and his companion stood a few feet away, appearing perfectly fine, if a bit waterlogged.

Cora gave the man a look of disbelief, then shook her head and started walking toward the docks.

Adam followed. It wasn't easy, moving through the water while fully dressed, but neither was it impossible, and standing around waiting seemed pointless. The other passengers soon did the same, slowly wading their way out of the pool. Whatever mysterious creature had caused them to capsize, it didn't resurface.

Athletic Cora didn't need any assistance. She hauled herself up onto the dock and shook water from her skirts, then extended a hand to Adam. He shook his head and instead helped one of the other ladies, lifting her out of the water to the workers on the dock, who steadied her on her feet, then led her to a bench to sit. Others soon followed to sit with her.

The couple who had been in front of Cora and Adam snuggled close, comforting one another.

Cora paced the dock, water dripping from her clothing, soggy tendrils of hair tumbling about her shoulders. Her hat still floated in the pool, but she showed no sign of caring.

"Are you well?" Adam asked her. "You're not hurt, are you?"

She paused. "No, of course not. Are you?"

"No, no. Just wet."

"Good." She paced to the edge of the dock, frowning down at the water, arms crossed beneath her breasts.

Adam's breath hitched. Good lord. With the way the wet fabric clung to her, he could see the outline of her corset and the curve where her bosom swelled over the top of it. He dragged his gaze up to her face. Droplets of water lingered on her eyelashes. The moisture on her lips made it appear she'd just been kissed.

Help.

"We, uh, that is..."

Cora tipped her head to one side. "Are you sure you're all right? Do you need to sit down a moment?"

"No, I'm, fine, truly. We ought to get you back to your hotel so you can change into new clothes." It wouldn't help him much. His imagination was too vivid, and he'd already been flung down the path of inappropriate thoughts. Her comfort and well-being, however, needed to be a priority.

"Oh." She lifted one shoulder and let it drop. "It's warm today. I'll dry soon enough." She shielded her eyes from the glaring sunlight. "I don't see anything in the pool. Did you get a look at the thing that knocked us over?"

"No." He honestly hadn't given it a thought since climbing from the water. Too distracted by her. "I glimpsed the tail of what looked like a large dragon, but only for an instant." He scanned the water. A crew was righting the overturned boat, but otherwise the pool was calm. With the ride at a halt, no water ran down the ramp, and the current had slowed to a near standstill. "Right now I don't even see signs of disturbance in the water."

"Nor do I. But I know this: large dragons don't appear accidentally in a pool and then just happen to ram a boatload of passengers."

Adam blinked at her. "You think this was, what? An attack?"

She turned to look him directly in the eye. "Do you have any enemies?"

He rocked back on his heels. "What? No!"

"I think you might. Your firing the other day doesn't sit well with me. Why was Hampton there? And how could he not have known about me after my demonstration? It feels to me as if he arranged to catch me using the machine and turn that against you."

"And you think now he's sending dragons to attack me?" Adam couldn't fathom the idea. He was a nobody. Just an engineer. What possible reason could anyone have for wishing him harm? This entire incident hadn't even been especially dangerous to his person. More of an inconvenience. "Why would Hampton or anyone do that?"

"I don't know. I only know the circumstances are suspicious."

"Sir? Miss?" Adam and Cora turned toward the dock worker. "Steam cars are arriving to drive you to your hotels, or wherever you need to go. If you'll follow me, please?"

Adam gestured for Cora to go first. "You should go change. We can talk later. Where and when would you like to meet?"

"Oh, no. If someone is trying to hurt you, I'm not letting you out of my sight. Not until we have some answers."

Adam stepped close enough to whisper. "Cora, I cannot go to your hotel room. I'm not going to risk getting you in trouble."

"I don't need to go to the hotel. I told you, I'll dry

eventually. What about you? Are you cold? Should we return to your room?"

"No." He rubbed his temple. "Fine, fine. Your hotel. I'll... stand guard in the hall while you change."

"We can discuss that later. Let's go. Someone has ruined my fun day at the fair and is trying to trouble you, if not harm you. I'm not going to be satisfied until I know who and why."

Adam followed her, not saying anything, his mind churning. He truly had no enemies. Hampton was rid of him. Nothing else made sense. Unless...

A shiver started at the base of Adam's neck and ran all the way down his spine. Unless the attack had been aimed not at him, but at Cora. She had the right idea. Propriety be damned. He wasn't letting her out of his sight.

10

Excerpt of a letter from Miss Cora Maxwell to Mr. Adam Levett, dated June. 27, 1904

The papers are still blathering about the Dynalux deal. I know you are a fan of electrical power, but have you ever used luxene in your inventions? Do you think it will ever truly power automobiles?

Sept. 6, afternoon

"**H**AVE YOU EVER KISSED A WOMAN, Mr. Levett?" Cora wondered.

"I can say with one hundred percent certainty that he has."

Cora jumped and whirled around. She hadn't meant for anyone to hear that particular statement. She'd believed the hall outside Levett's hotel room to be entirely empty or she wouldn't have been talking to herself. Mr. Doyle, however, had apparently snuck up on her.

"I've seen it," Doyle continued. "Frustrated because he hasn't kissed you yet?"

"No," she blurted.

"Uh-huh. Want me to nudge him for you?"

"No." This answer was firm. The last thing Cora needed was outside interference. Her romantic life was confusing enough as it was. "But maybe you could poke your head into the room and check that he's all right. He's been in there a long time."

She couldn't help but worry for him. He'd been in those wet clothes for over an hour, and his suit was heavy and wool, not the light cotton she preferred. They really ought to have come here first.

Doyle cocked a blond eyebrow, then shrugged and slotted a key into the lock. "I'll hurry him up."

"Thank you."

Cora walked a small circle, following the pattern in the rug beneath her feet. Her skirt swirled around her boots. She'd replaced her sodden outfit with one of the sleeveless dresses that she preferred for shooting, and plaited her wet hair into a pair of simple braids. No gloves, no hat, no parasol. She would draw "looks" from rigid society matrons and stuffy gentlemen, but no matter. Times changed, fashions changed. It was the way of the world.

Levett would no doubt appear in another nice suit, though possibly with a skipped or misaligned button somewhere. She wished he'd appear in nothing but trousers and rolled-up shirtsleeves. Or maybe in shorts and a sleeveless top, like the track-and-field athletes wore. Cora would love to see his arms and legs exposed.

The possibility of getting even a glimpse was slim. She'd practically had to drag him up to her hotel room, even with the assurance he could stand outside the door. Which had led her to wondering if the reason he hadn't kissed her last night was simply nerves. Maybe he didn't know how. She'd never heard him mention a current or former sweetheart in his letters.

Doyle had shot down that theory, though. Unless he was lying? Men probably weren't supposed to admit to things such as not knowing how to kiss a woman. Doyle could have said that to hide his friend's lack of knowledge. Or to fluster Cora. Or...

Her stomach dropped. Oh, no. What if Doyle was involved in the boating incident? She'd let him walk right past her, and now he was alone with Levett. While she stood here like a fool, fantasizing about naked body parts.

Cora raced to the door, lifting her fist to pound on it. She'd managed only a single thud before the door swung open, revealing a now-dry Levett. Doyle stood behind him, not looking in the least murderous or threatening. The best criminals, Cora suspected, looked equally trustworthy.

"Miss Maxwell," Levett said, smoothing down his wavy hair with his fingers. "So sorry to keep you waiting. I was, um, washing up. The pool water, you know. Quite filthy."

Behind him Doyle did the skeptical one-eyebrow raise again. How did he do that? And just what *had* Levett been doing? Clearly his friend didn't believe him.

Levett had changed into a white shirt, with a navy vest and matching trousers. No coat. Well, that was a step in the right direction. A red bow tie hung around his neck but wasn't knotted. Cora reached up and whisked it away, tossing it past him into the room.

"Don't bother with that. Let's go."

"Um..."

Doyle prodded Levett from the room before he could protest further. Levett frowned at his friend, then shrugged. "Doyle, tell Miss Maxwell what you were telling me."

Doyle's mouth hitched in a wry smile. "Well, there I was, attempting to woo our sad trickle of customers in the AutomaTech booth, when word comes along of a mishap on the Pike. A loose dragon, they say. Escaped from the Palace of Luxene, upended a boat on the Shoot the Chutes ride, soaked and terrified ladies, utter mayhem. Naturally, I hurried back here to discover if Levett had been involved."

Levet turned both his hands palm upward. "I still don't understand why you think I'd be involved."

"Adam," Doyle sighed. "You're always involved. You're attracted to trouble like flies are attracted to shit."

"Don't swear. There's a lady right in front of you."

Doyle shrugged. "Eh. She doesn't mind."

Cora grinned. She desperately hoped Doyle wasn't out to get Adam, because she liked him.

"Back to my point," he continued. "We'd barely been at AutomaTech for a month when you nearly burned down the office with that newfangled food-warmer invention."

"I left instructions!" Levett protested. "It's not my fault people don't read."

"And then the flying bicycle episode."

Levett folded his arms across his chest and huffed. "I told Rawley to his face it was a prototype. Anyone who enters a race with a vehicle that's never been built and tested before doesn't get my sympathies when he crashes."

Cora gave Levett a quizzical look. "You haven't told me that story yet."

"The bicycle works now," was his only answer. He scowled at Doyle.

"You're always involved," Doyle repeated. "So I assumed you would be involved in this too. And I was right. Now, tell me your side."

"Something rammed the boat from underneath and capsized it," Cora explained, when Levett said nothing. "We didn't get a good look at what it was. But the whole incident was suspicious. The rumors are saying a dragon escaped from the Palace of Luxene?"

"That's what I heard."

"We'll start there, then. Shall we, Mr. Levett?"

Levett sighed. "Yes. And hopefully we can prove it was no more than a strange accident."

Doyle shook his head. "Just be careful, okay? I have to

get back to work. Try not to draw attention to yourself. If Hampton finds out you're holed up in my room on company dollars, he'll be mad as a hornet and twice as mean."

"Then don't mention me. Or the Electro-Flex. Or his firefighting airship."

Doyle cringed. "The one you told him was 'hastily designed'?"

Adam had had nothing to do with the project, but he'd had a brief glimpse at the plans. The ship was to be AutomaTech's foray into the business of large machines. The reveal, originally scheduled for spring, had been repeatedly pushed back until everyone had assumed it would never happen.

"It was. Have you seen it? Has he been able to present it here at the fair? I rest my case."

"See?" Doyle looked at Cora and waved a hand at Levett. "Trouble."

Adam fidgeted with his glasses. "If this becomes a problem for you, I can move out."

"Sure. Maybe you can stay with Miss Maxwell instead."

Levett's face turned a shade of greyish-green. "That is… not funny."

"Wasn't joking." Doyle clapped him on the shoulder. "Take care." He locked his door and sauntered off.

Levett turned to Cora. "Er, the Palace of Luxene?" he asked. He started down the hall, keeping a bit of distance between them. She sighed and followed, missing the easy companionship they'd begun the day with.

"Yes."

· · · ⟶ · · ·

"Cleaning rats for home and office!"

Cora winced. "Not that again."

The Palace of Luxene lay between the Palace of Electricity and the Pike, lending some plausibility to the theory of an escaped dragon turning up in the water chute ride. The large entry doors stood wide open, and dragons roamed the corridors, not all of them tethered. A few flew around overhead. Cora stepped over the cleaning rat as it sucked up bits of shredded paper.

"I don't think that story makes sense," she murmured to Levett. When she leaned close, he edged away. Drat. All this turmoil had apparently ruined his desire to kiss her.

"Why not?" he asked.

"These luxene-powered dragons are small. Almost everything fueled by luxene is. A small dragon couldn't have tipped the boat. You're the engineer. Can you see anything here that could do it?"

Adam pursed his lips. "Strength and leverage are the key points. The tipping dragon, for lack of a better term, could have been extremely large, pushing the boat on sheer mass. Or it could have been smaller, but made from strong materials. The easiest way to tip the boat would be for it to brace itself against the bottom of the pool and push upward. It could be smallish, but with long, extendable legs in that case. What if what we saw wasn't a tail but a tentacle?"

"So we look for an octopus?"

"Maybe. But I've never worked with luxene. I don't actually know the capabilities of the fuel outside of what the papers and scientific journals report. The Dynalux claim is that they'll soon run automobiles on it. It's possible we might find a large dragon here."

"Then we should begin by walking about and observing." Cora gazed up into his eyes. "Like a strolling couple?"

"Yes." He looked quickly away. "We'll pretend we're out for a friendly jaunt and ask a few questions."

The task could have been enjoyable, if Adam's words had held true. To Cora's chagrin, by "friendly" he apparently meant "like causal and indifferent acquaintances." He didn't offer her his arm, and he kept almost an entire person's width away from her as they walked. More than once, another visitor slipped between them, thinking they'd left a deliberate path. Levett hardly even looked at her. What was wrong with him?

"Stop here," she instructed, deliberately closing the space between them. This was ridiculous. Maybe he didn't wish to kiss her anymore, but he didn't need to act as if he couldn't stand the sight of her.

He didn't move away, but he took a steadying breath.

The exhibit in front of them had been built to resemble a section of a mine. Inside, sprayers on tall poles sent a steady mist of water at the greenish rock walls.

"Says here the luxene in raw ore form can be dangerously explosive," Levett said, paraphrasing the explanatory sign in front of him. "The sprayers keep the mines moist, allowing for safe extraction and transportation."

Cora grasped his elbow and tugged him toward the next section of the exhibit. "In these vats, the ore is slowly stirred and dissolved in precisely the correct proportion of water to produce a stable and useful fuel." She glanced up at Levett. "I had no idea. No one bothers to tell you these things."

"Cassidy Mining is currently the only luxene mining operation in existence," Levett replied, reading the next plaque over. "The pure luxene is sold to a number of distributors for bottling and sale to the public."

"Do you folks have any questions?"

Cora looked up—and up—into the face of an enormously tall man in a tidy gray suit.

"Owen Cassidy," he introduced himself. "Owner of Cassidy Mining. I ought to be able to answer any question you have."

"You discovered luxene!" Levett blurted. "What was it about the material that made you think it was a viable fuel source? Do you truly think it can be something beyond a niche fuel for small dragons? Can you give me some concrete examples of what advantages it might hold over electrical power?"

Mr. Cassidy's eyes widened in surprise. "Uh, which question would you like me to answer first, Mr...?"

Levett's eyelashes fluttered several times behind his spectacles. "Oh, um, sorry." He held out a hand. "Levett. Adam Levett. Formerly of AutomaTech. Inventor of the Electro-Flex."

Mr. Cassidy didn't appear to have heard of Levett or his invention, but he shook hands and nodded politely.

"Actually, Mr. Cassidy, we are interested in learning about luxene and dragons," Cora said, trying to steer the conversation to their purpose for being here. "Does it only fuel small ones, or can it fuel something larger? The ones that pull carriages, perhaps?"

Cassidy shook his head. "You'll be better off talking to the manufacturers about that. I only supply the fuel. They use it. And the distributors, of course. I believe Dynalux is the most diligent in their efforts to put luxene to multiple uses."

"Thank you." She reached to take Levett's arm, but this time he hardly seemed to notice.

"About the luxene versus electricity question," he began, his gaze fixed on Cassidy.

Cora released him and stepped away. Levett had fallen into a scientific reverie. Pulling him out of it would take more effort than it was worth.

"I'll be back later," she told him, though his preoccupied nod suggested she was wasting her breath.

Cora skirted around the Tagget Industries exhibit, a surprisingly unadorned area, with multiple teletic devices and shelves of small machines, all available for visitors to touch and play with. The space was packed with people laughing and smiling, enjoying the hands-on technology. AutomaTech could learn a thing or two. What were a few potential broken machines compared to a whole crowd leaving an exhibit happy and with a positive impression of the company? Cora failed to smother her smug smile at that thought.

A few exhibits further, she spied what she wanted: a booth full of dragons, resembling dozens of different real-life animals.

Smack in the middle of the display was an octopus, eight two-foot long tentacles dangling from a melon-sized body.

"This is lovely," she said to the pale-faced, whiskered man who stood nearby, wearing a badge that declared him an employee of "Home Dragons, Inc." Levett wasn't the only person who failed to invent interesting names. "Does it really swim?"

"Oh, yes," the man replied. "Quite fascinating to watch." He eyed her bare, tanned arms. "Great fun for playing in a lake or a stream. Perfect for an outdoor enthusiast."

"It's a bit small." Cora gave an exaggerated sigh. "What I'm looking for is one strong enough to pull my boat, like a carriage dragon for the water. And I don't trust electrical machines. Always starting fires. Do you have any luxene-powered dragons with enough horsepower for my purposes?"

He shook his head. "No, miss. All the larger dragons run on steam. You'll be wanting to go to the Palace of Transportation for that."

"Thank you." She gave the man a nod and continued on.

Two more manufacturers of luxene-powered creatures and devices corroborated these findings. By the time she returned to retrieve Levett—who was animatedly arguing with Mr. Cassidy about the advantages of electrical appliances—Cora was convinced that no dragon escaping from this Palace could have overturned their boat in such a fashion.

Adam didn't see her approach, too wrapped up in extolling the wonders of batteries and portable electronics. Mr. Cassidy nodded along, his tight jaw suggesting he wanted to get back to work but was too polite to disrupt Levett's enthusiastic oration.

Cora had little to no interest in batteries, but hearing Adam speak on the subject made her smile and listen regardless. He was enchanting. His eyes sparkled. His hands gestured animatedly to punctuate his points. This was the world he loved, and seeing him so immersed in it made her heart thump a little oddly. He was so alive, so very much himself, having forgotten the rest of the world existed, much less what it thought of him.

Only when he reached a stopping point in his explanations did he notice her presence.

"Oh, Cora. Er, Miss Maxwell. I'm sorry to keep you waiting. The subject of batteries came up, and—"

"Quite all right. Shall we walk on and leave Mr. Cassidy to his work?"

"Yes, of course." Levett nodded to the taller man. "Lovely to meet you. Sorry if I talked your ear off." He allowed Cora to steer him away, and when they were alone said, "My apologies. I didn't mean to get so distracted. Did you discover something?"

"None of the dragons here are large or strong enough to have tipped that boat. The rumor is wrong. Perhaps an outright lie."

"Damn," he cursed. "Oh, pardon my language."

"It's only a word, Adam. I'm not going to burst into flames upon hearing it. I'm not an offended-by-swearing sort of person. Please don't stress yourself over it. Besides, I think the situation merits a strong reaction."

"I'll say. If someone has lied about it being an accident, I can only conclude that it was intentional."

"Agreed. Which means we stick together and look for anything suspicious. No more splitting up, not even to talk science. Or sports. Or anything. Never apart, always watching one another's back. That's how friends handle this sort of thing, right?"

"Right." Levett took a step back, his weight shifting nervously. "But what about at night?"

Cora bit her lower lip. That was the trouble, wasn't it? Especially given her unruly body and his hot-then-cold reactions to her. Still, better to have to struggle through those issues than leave him to someone who might cause him bodily harm.

"There are two beds in my hotel room," she offered.

11

Excerpt of a letter from Mr. Adam Levett to Miss Cora Maxwell, dated April 4, 1904

My Dear Miss Maxwell,

Thank you for the newspaper clipping and photo. I am thrilled to see you competing and excelling. The Indianapolis Archery Club is lucky to have you, and I am delighted that they featured you in the paper. I have tucked the article into my notes for the Electro-Flex, and it will forever be a treasured reminder of our friendship.

Sept. 6, evening

ADAM SLAMMED A LATCH ON HIS TRUNK closed, ignoring Doyle's disapproving frown.

"I didn't mean you should up and leave," Doyle insisted.

"I know."

"It's a bad idea."

"I know." Adam closed the second latch and rose to his feet. "It's a terrible idea." He glanced out the open door to where Cora waited, in sight, but out of earshot, assuming he kept his voice down. "I can hardly look at her without wanting to—"

"Give yourself a rub-off while she paces the hallway outside?"

Adam glared at his friend, because his only other alternative was to cringe in embarrassment. God, he hoped Cora hadn't guessed what he'd done. He hastily returned to the relevant subject. "I don't know what else to do. I can't leave her alone if someone is trying to hurt her."

"What if it's not about her? What if it's *you*?"

"It's not me."

Doyle let out a long breath. "I don't know. People are whispering. Rawley practically chortled with glee when he heard what happened. I don't like it, the way you were sacked. Something's not right."

Adam shook his head and grabbed the handle on the end of his trunk, dragging it toward the door. "Just go to bed. There's no other choice. I have to keep Miss Maxwell safe."

"You do remember the part where she's a champion with a deadly weapon, don't you?"

Cora's head swiveled toward them. "Of course he does. That's why he's agreed to stay with me. He knows I can protect him if needed."

Doyle gave her a flirtatious grin. "Well, I can certainly see the appeal of that. The only thing that sounds better than having a fierce lady friend defend me would be sparring with her." He winked. Cora laughed.

Adam's stomach clenched. He suppressed the sudden urge to make Doyle do most of the work as they lugged Adam's belongings down the stairs and out to the waiting carriage. Dammit, he was driving himself mad. He didn't *want* to be jealous.

But he wanted that easy rapport with Cora. He wanted to flirt with her. The trouble was, he didn't know how to do that without overstepping the boundaries of their friendship. He couldn't break her trust, he couldn't push her into something unwanted, and he couldn't ruin what they'd developed over a year's worth of correspondence.

The brass and iron horse hitched to the carriage stomped a hoof on the pavement and blew steam from its nostrils. Even machines were impatient tonight. Doyle helped Cora up into the carriage, bowing over her hand and bidding her a gallant farewell. It was all Adam could do not to grab his friend by the lapels and order him to stop being so blasted charming.

You're making me look bad!

That wasn't true. Adam was making himself look bad. He clambered into the carriage, suppressing a groan of frustration. Cora gave the driver her direction and they started off, the horse-dragon hissing and blowing more steam as it clopped down the road, away from the spectacle of the fair, toward the city beyond.

A long silence ensued, until at last Cora inquired, "Have you known Mr. Doyle long?"

Oh, no. Was she romantically interested in Doyle? If she was, Adam would have to help foster the relationship. It only made sense. He was friends with them both. A natural bridge between the two of them. He didn't know if he'd be able to stand it.

"Years," Adam replied. His throat felt scratchy. He needed a drink of water. Or maybe something stronger. "We met in college. Both ended up working for AutomaTech."

"And you find him trustworthy, then?"

"Of course. I mean, he's a horrendous flirt, but—"

"Well, that's not very relevant."

Adam frowned at her. "It's not?"

"Not unless you mean he leads women on and makes promises he has no intention of keeping. I hadn't seen any indication he'd do such a thing, but behavior of that sort would be an indication of villainy."

"Villainy?" Adam choked the word out.

"I know he's your friend," Cora said soothingly. "And I don't want him to be a villain. But it's important we consider whether it's a possibility he was involved in this morning's troubles."

"This… what?" Adam rubbed his temple as his brain attempted to shift direction. "Do you mean you're concerned he might have had something to do with that dragon in the water ride?"

"Yes. What did you think I was talking about?"

Adam's hand dropped to his lap. "I thought you were worried he would attempt to seduce you."

Her green eyes widened. Then she laughed. "Seduce me? Even if he wanted to, I'm not interested."

"But then why the flirtations?"

Cora's nose wrinkled in confusion. "*You* brought up flirtations. I thought you might mean he'd done something inappropriate with a lady or ladies in the past. Hence, villainy."

"No, I meant…" Adam slapped his palm across his face again. "Christ, I'm an idiot. Sorry for the swearing. I meant he flirts often and casually. In case you thought all his smiling and winking implied something more. I didn't want you to misinterpret it, if you were, uh, drawn to him."

"Well, I just told you I'm not, so hopefully that will ease your mind. And I know I've complained to you about how difficult romance can be, but I'm not *completely* naive. I don't mind Doyle's friendly flirting."

Friendly flirting. Yes, Adam supposed that's what it was. Maybe he could friendly flirt too. Stop worrying about consequences and just tease and laugh with her the way he wanted to. His heart raced. Surely this fell into the category of Very Bad Idea. Especially when he was spending the night in her hotel room.

The cab trundled on, quieter now on dirt streets lit only by the occasional gas lamp. Adam stared at the shuttered buildings as they rolled by. Unadorned brick, most of them. Simple and sturdy, and tiny in comparison to the grand palaces they'd just left behind. He hadn't been outside the Exposition in two months. So long that the mundanity of real life had become a curiosity. The normal had become the fantastical, which only added to the outlandishness of sleeping in the same room as the woman he'd been pining over for at least half a year.

When they arrived at the hotel, Adam paid the driver before Cora could protest. Yes, he was out of a job, but he had savings. He wasn't about to make her pay for hauling him and his belongings around.

"Goodnight, sir, ma'am," the driver said. "Hope you enjoyed your stay at the fair."

He thinks we're leaving. Together. He probably thinks we're married.

Adam's palms began to sweat. This was so far beyond a bad idea. He was going to ruin Cora's reputation. She could lose her place in the Olympic competition. Worse things had happened to women for so-called 'immoral behavior.'

"Cora, what are we going to tell people?" he whispered. "To explain why I'm here?"

"Nothing. No one cares. They don't know us." She raised a hand to catch the attention of a porter. "Excuse me, sir, could you carry my luggage up to my room? It's room 312."

"Certainly, ma'am." He and one other man hurried over to pick up Adam's belongings and carried them off into the hotel.

"See? No one is questioning anything. I'll give them a good tip, everyone will be happy, and that's all."

Adam shook his head. "This is how you became an archery champion, isn't it? You assume you're going to win. You can't envision losing."

She motioned for him to follow her inside. "I've lost plenty of times."

"But that's only a step in your process. In your future, you always win. There's a 'someday' hanging out in front of you where you're the champion, accepting the winner's trophy."

"Medal."

He blinked. "Excuse me?"

"This way." Cora nodded at the stairs. "They're giving out medals for the Olympics. Some trophies, too, but they have special medals. Gold for the winner, silver for second, bronze for third."

"Oh. Okay, then. You picture yourself receiving a gold medal."

"Yes, I suppose I do." A grin spread across her face. "I'll be smiling. So hard it hurts. And maybe crying a little, too. You'll be in the stands nearby, cheering."

"No. I'll be leaping over the rail and running to give you the biggest hug you've ever received."

Cora froze. Adam stumbled to a halt. He'd spoken without thinking, his vivid imagination seeing the events unfold in perfect color. The inappropriateness of the comment—or of such behavior—hadn't even entered his mind until it was too late.

He opened his mouth to apologize, but Cora was staring at him and leaning in, as if she wanted to kiss him. Impossible. It had to be more absurd imaginings.

"I would like that," she said, softly. "It would be a lovely way to celebrate."

Yes, lovely. So very lovely. So very kissable.

The sound of footsteps above them broke the moment. Adam and Cora stepped to the side to allow the man coming down the stairs to pass, then continued up, neither attempting to continue the conversation.

Had he made things awkward? He'd made things awkward. Why was he so bad at this? It wasn't as if he was an untried youth. He was no Casanova, but he'd wooed women before with at least moderate success. Cora, though, turned him into a babbling fool. And the last thing in the world he wanted was to ruin what they already had.

The porters had his luggage waiting outside Cora's room.

As promised, she tipped them generously, and they departed with smiles and no questions asked. Cora unlocked the door, grabbed one end of the trunk, and hauled it inside. Not seeing any other choice, Adam assisted. Once inside, she closed the door and locked it behind them.

The tiny click of the lock thundered in Adam's chest. He was alone with her. Entirely alone with no one around to see, no one around to know. Cora set the key atop a chest of drawers and walked right up to him, closer even than she'd been on the stairs.

"The bed on the right is mine." She waved a hand. "Feel free to take the other one. The bathing chambers are down the hall just past the stairs. My clothes are all in the wardrobe, but I can make room for your things if you'd like."

"Thank you. I'll, uh, step out to give you privacy any time you like. And if I ever make you uncomfortable—"

"You won't. But *you* seem a bit uncomfortable."

"I'm fine." He shifted his weight. She was so close. He could lean in and kiss her at any moment. The wanting was driving him mad.

"You're sure? Because you look nervous."

Adam forced his body to still. "Not nervous. Unsettled." *Aroused. Ravenous. Unable to do anything about it.*

"Does the impropriety bother you that much? Is it really so terrible to be here?"

"No. It's never terrible being with you." Torturous, perhaps, but not terrible.

A blush stole over her cheeks. "Thank you."

"You're welcome." Adam took a step backward, hoping to relieve some of the tension strangling his body. "We should turn in. It's late. Shall I wait in the hall while you change?"

"Stop." Once more she closed the space between them. "You're doing it again."

"Doing what?"

"Pulling away from me after it looked like… well…" She took a deep breath. "Can I ask you a question?"

"Of course."

"Please tell the truth. Do you want to kiss me, Mr. Levett?"

Adam's breath hitched. He swayed toward Cora. "Yes," he whispered. "More than anything."

12

Excerpt of a letter from Miss Cora Maxwell to Mr. Adam Levett, dated October 12, 1903

When I'm truly focused, the rest of the world dissolves away. All that remains is myself and the target. & the moment I release the arrow, I know. It's struck true.

CORA HAD FORGOTTEN HOW FAST Levett could move. The words, "Kiss me," were hardly out of her mouth before he backed her into the wall, devastating her with the searing heat of his kiss. His body covered hers and his hands clamped over her wrists, pinning her in place. The absent-minded engineer had some fierceness in him, and her body thrilled to the force of it. She was utterly at his mercy, yet entirely safe. The heady combination set her mind reeling and her skin prickling.

In the past, she'd found it slobbery and intrusive when Benedict had tried putting his tongue in her mouth, but when Adam attempted the same she allowed it without hesitation. The kiss was wet, yes, but also fiery, exciting, and stunningly arousing. She opened more fully, and he moved deeper. Tasting. Teasing.

Cora began to experiment, copying his movements, dragging her tongue across his lower lip, then plunging it into his mouth to spar with his. He groaned into her, pushing her more firmly against the wall, thrusting the hard length of his arousal against her.

Hell and damnation. She was probably supposed to clobber him for such behavior, but all she did was whimper in helpless pleasure. She liked this surprise side of him. Powerful. Aggressive. As if nothing could stand between him and his desire to kiss her senseless.

Cora squirmed against him, craving this merge of bodies. Her breasts had turned madly sensitive where they rubbed him, and the junction of her thighs was growing damp.

Levett dragged his mouth from hers, kissing down her neck. His fingers skimmed over the insides of her wrists, sending ticklish shivers all along her arms. The room had become unbearably hot, even in her lightweight dress.

"Adam," she gasped.

"Cora." He sucked at her skin where her neck met her shoulder, tugging the wide strap of her sleeveless dress aside and letting his tongue stroke the flesh he exposed. Again he rocked his hips into her. "God, Cora, I want you so much."

She wanted him, too. It was madness. She actually wanted to tear all her clothes off and feel his hands on her bare skin. Usually she cursed the illogical swells of desire she felt for attractive men. Tonight she was embracing one.

With his right hand busy tugging at the strap of her dress, Cora had one arm left dangling freely. Not knowing what else to do, she began to touch him, running her fingers along his side, around to his back, then sliding down to the curve of his bottom. He had quite the nicely shaped rear end. Cora couldn't help giving it a squeeze.

Adam jumped. His mouth pulled away from her neck and he straightened up, releasing her and backing slowly away. He adjusted his spectacles.

"S-sorry." His eyes were dark with desire and his skin flushed. The bulge of his rigid shaft strained the fabric of his trousers. Cora trembled with the memory of the feel of it against her belly. "I let myself get carried away. That was completely inappropriate and I apologize."

"I liked it," Cora replied. Her voice had a low, sensual purr to it. "It was exciting. Did you think I wasn't enjoying it?"

"No, I…" He fidgeted with his glasses again. "I don't want to take advantage of you. We're friends. You should be able to trust me."

Cora almost laughed. "Of course I trust you." There was no way she would have let him trap her against the wall the way he had if she didn't trust him. But this was Levett. He listened and he cared. If she was uncomfortable, fearful, or simply uninterested, he would stop.

He stared at her, shaking his head. "I was all but ravishing you up against the wall. You invited me to your room out of friendship, and that was… not friendly."

Cora folded her arms across her chest. "Friends can't kiss?"

"Uh…"

"It seems to me you are highly attracted to me. Is that true?"

Levett sighed. "Yes."

"And I know for a fact I'm highly attracted to you. Setting aside any social pressures to behave in certain ways, why shouldn't we be allowed to experiment with that attraction?"

"We're friends," he repeated, as if that were a legitimate argument. "But if I kiss you then we're, well, I don't know exactly."

"Still friends," Cora declared. "I see no reason why a kiss would mean we can't be friends. We'll just be friends plus something else. Friends with kissing. Friends with… perquisites."

Adam gawked at her, twice opening his mouth to speak then closing it before he finally managed to say, "Your argument is highly compelling. Which probably means I'm feverish. I ought to take myself off to bed immediately." He took two hurried strides toward the unused bed. "I'll, uh, sleep on it. Figuratively, I meant. The idea. But literally on the bed also." He winced. "Never mind." He dropped heavily onto the bed, falling backward and staring up at the ceiling. Heaving another sigh, he kicked off his shoes, yanked the coverlet up over himself, and rolled over.

"Aren't you going to change out of your suit?"

"No." The word was slightly muffled by his pillow. "Good night."

Cora sank onto the edge of her own bed. "Good night." In this, at least, he was probably right. A bit of time to recover and think things over was only sensible. With some distance between them, her mind had begun to emerge from the fog of lust. What on earth had happened?

Ravishing you up against the wall, he had said. And she'd been entirely amenable to ravishment. She still was, though now she was wondering why he had such a powerful effect on her.

"Maybe we need the kissing," she mused aloud. "Maybe indulging in it will satisfy the physical attraction. Which is why it's good that we're friends. When it burns out, we can still be friends, only without the additional perquisites."

Levett made a noise, but Cora couldn't tell whether it was agreement or disagreement.

"Isn't that what people say? That passion is a fleeting thing?" She shrugged. "Or maybe not. I'm rather terrible at romance, as I'm sure you know from my letters. I'm sorry, I'm not letting you sleep."

With nothing to do but turn in for the night, Cora scurried off to the washroom to scrub her face and change into her nightgown. Babbling inanely at Levett wasn't going to help anything.

She ran a finger over her lips, finding them still sensitive from the kissing. The washroom mirror was old and cracked, but she took some time to study her reflection as best she could, examining her neck and shoulder for evidence of Levett's attentions. The red mark could have been from him, or perhaps only from the strap of her dress.

She tugged the edge of the nightgown up to cover it and turned away from the mirror. Better not to think about it. Thinking only led to wanting, and that would only lead her into distraction.

Looking back on those few, frenzied minutes, Cora wasn't sure whether she'd done anything right. Should she have touched him more? Less? Kissed harder? Not surrendered so easily to his desire? To be frank, she didn't have any idea if there was a right way to do this sort of thing or not. The few salacious books she'd managed to read hadn't actually gone into much detail. And she'd been too busy with her archery to hunt down anything racier. Besides, why bother, when none of the men around seemed compatible with her?

Back in the bedroom, she extinguished the lights and lay wide awake, thinking about Adam across the room in the other bed. She would be dreaming of his kisses, she was sure of it. When they left this room in the morning, though, she would have to take more care. In his arms, she'd forgotten everything. The fair, the Olympics, the possibility of an enemy attacking them. She couldn't afford to forget.

Part of her wanted to tell Levett to leave the Exposition and return home. To not bother staying to watch her compete. It wasn't worth possible harm.

Cora rolled over and tried to fluff up her pillow. He probably wouldn't listen. And she was selfishly glad for it. She didn't want him to leave. They'd only just met in person and already the idea of not seeing him caused a pang in her chest. Another matter to puzzle over. So many questions.

She tossed and turned for hours, thoughts swirling in her brain. When morning came at long last, it brought no new answers.

13

Excerpt of a letter from Mr. Adam Levett to Miss Cora Maxwell, dated November 7, 1903

Electricity is the future! So many practical applications. So many ways to generate electrical power. Forget steam engines. Forget luxene. I want an electric motorcar. (Not that I can afford a motorcar at present, but it's a dream of mine.) Perhaps someday I'll take you on a ride.

Sept. 7, afternoon

𝒜DAM REMOVED HIS GLASSES and scrubbed a hand across his face. God, what a day. Between fearing for Cora's well-being and berating himself for his behavior the night before, he'd worn himself ragged. And he'd hardly done anything besides walk the fair and watch Cora at her daily activities.

She'd spent an hour that morning in the hotel room, working through a series of exercises with her rubber bands. He'd watched the process in absolute silence, trying not to ogle her like a lecher. Fortunately, it wasn't all wasted time. He'd jotted several pages worth of notes for possible complementary products to the Electro-Flex. Ideas for his athletic training devices business continued to flow.

Adam paced the fifty yards to the target to retrieve the last of Cora's arrows. Helping her fetch them had done little to relieve his stress, but at least it kept his body moving. Without that, he would have worn a rut in the dirt from anxious pacing.

He glanced again in the direction of the athletic field, still convinced Thompson or another angry competitor would appear at any moment. An Olympic judge might wander over and disqualify her for some unknown reason. Someone from the Exposition management might throw them out and rescind their entry passes.

So far none of these things had happened, but Adam couldn't shake his fear for her. She'd worked so damn hard to be here. For this chance to compete on a world-wide stage and show that women's athletics did deserve to be celebrated as much as men's. She belonged here, and he was prepared to fight anyone who tried to stand in the way of that.

"Are you okay?" Cora yanked out one of her arrows and waved it in front of Adam's face. "You seem distracted. Did you think of a new idea for a machine?"

"Er." Adam blinked and reached to pluck an arrow for her. "No. I was thinking about other things. My lack of athletic ability."

"Oh, well, I'm sure that's mostly a lack of training. You're fit enough, and as I've said, you walk very fast. That's a good indicator of health and strength. You could learn a sport if you applied yourself."

"Mm-hmm." Really, he'd been thinking of his lack of ability to fight or chase off anyone who came after her. He was no knight in shining armor. Not even a knight in old rags. More like the king's scribe who never left the library.

Adam rolled his shoulders. The tension of standing around all day preparing his mind and body for danger had left him aching. He needed something relaxing to free him from this unending cycle of paranoia. Something highly public, where no one would dare do Cora any harm. And no rides or machines that could malfunction. A nice dinner, perhaps.

"You've been working hard today," he said, before he could think better of it. "Let me take you out to dinner tonight. You deserve a good meal, and maybe a glass of wine."

Cora's eyebrows lifted.

Yes, I just asked you on a date. No, it wasn't a good idea.

"I know what you're thinking," he added hastily. "I shouldn't be spending money on things like this when I'm unemployed."

He was pretty sure that was *not* what she'd been thinking, but it made a good topic of argument that had nothing to do with his feelings for her, their mutual attraction, or the absolutely insane way he'd kissed her last night. He wanted this. Needed this.

Adam had been careful all day not to touch her, while trying to prevent any flinching away or other signs of avoidance. Knowing now how eagerly she'd responded to his kiss, he couldn't let her think it had been some aberration, or that he didn't truly want her. Because if he had even the slimmest chance to win her, he wanted to take it.

Tonight, he would try wooing her. Starting with convincing her to join him for dinner. If their night together began to seem romantic, he'd know to continue on that path. And if not… The worst that would happen was they would have a lovely dinner together as friends.

"I promise, I have enough in my savings for one special dinner. Consider it an early celebration for your competition. I know you'll have less and less time to spare as the day draws nearer. We can even call it a business meeting. Discuss my plans to begin my own company and your ideas for technologies to include. And what to name them."

Adam bit the inside of his lip. Darn it all. He'd just turned his date into a business outing. Not romantic.

Cora's mouth twisted as she considered his words. "Very well. I'll let you buy me dinner. But only this once."

A quick ride on the Intramural Railway took them to the corner of the fair closest to Cora's hotel, where they made a brief stop to stow her archery equipment and freshen up for dinner.

In the men's washroom, Adam scoured his hands and face, shaved again, and dressed in his best suit, taking care not to miss any buttons. He scowled at his reflection. His tie was sloppy and his hair too long. Several more minutes of fussing did nothing to improve his appearance. It would have to do. Cora was probably waiting.

He rapped on the hotel room door, in case she hadn't finished dressing, but she opened it promptly and waved him inside. Adam swallowed hard, trying not to stare.

She'd changed out of her everyday dress into a slim, dark blue gown with a low, scooped neckline and tiny sleeves that sat almost off her shoulders. The ornamentation was simple—only ribbon trim and no fancy embroidery—but the fabric was satin, or maybe silk. Adam wasn't sure of the exact material, but it shimmered with each subtle movement of her body, clinging to her curves like a second skin.

A reddish mark was visible on her left shoulder. *His* mark. Damn. It had been hidden all day by her other dress, but now anyone could see it and guess what she'd been up to last night. And since Adam would be with her, they could also guess who was responsible.

He fought against the flare of arousal the sight of that small love bite stirred in him. He longed to kiss it. To lave it with his tongue. To leave another, similar mark on her opposite shoulder. Or perhaps lower, where even this dress covered.

"Miss Maxwell." Adam made some approximation of a formal bow. "I am unable to properly convey your beauty in mere words. I can only say that you look nearly as splendid as you do with a bow in your hand."

A touch of pink highlighted Cora's cheeks as she laughed. "I was under the impression that most men would find me *more* beautiful this way."

Adam walked toward her. "Your dress certainly does highlight your, uh, physical attributes." His gaze wandered over her hips and breasts before he caught himself and looked up into her eyes. "I admit I am not immune."

Cora stepped close enough to touch him, reaching to straighten his tie. "I'm not immune, either. You look dashing this evening. The dark gray suit brings out the silvery tones in your eyes."

Adam automatically adjusted his spectacles. "I was not aware I had silvery tones."

Cora's mouth tilted up toward his. "Oh, yes. They sparkle in the right light."

"You sparkle too." He imagined her twirling in a room ablaze with electric lights. "I will be the object of much jealousy tonight."

If we make it out the door. If I don't just kiss you senseless right here, right now.

He bent to brush a feather-light kiss across her lips. "Shall we depart?"

Cora drew in a long breath and pulled away. "I suppose we should. Otherwise we might not get any dinner."

He would happily skip dinner for her. But considering how out of hand things had gotten the night before and his complete lack of preparedness, sticking to his original plan was the better option. Besides, the entire point was to woo her. To see if she was amenable to a romantic relationship, or if they were truly meant to be friends who happened to have a strong sexual pull between them.

When the door was locked behind them, Adam took her hand rather than offering his arm. Their fingers entwined, the movement feeling both natural and comfortable. Her palm was warm, her grip firm. Fingers calloused from holding the bowstring pressed into his skin.

His body thrilled to her touch, but their interlocked hands sparked something deeper in his chest. A sense of rightness. Happiness. Contentment. Her letters had the same effect on him. Proximity only magnified his reaction.

"Did you have a specific place in mind for this fancy dinner of yours?" Cora asked as they boarded a trolley bound for the fairgrounds. She held her skirts up almost to her knees so as not to trip over them, exposing the same sturdy brown boots she usually wore. Sensible for a 1200 acre fairground requiring extensive walking.

"I do," he replied. "Why don't you try to guess?"

As the journey progressed, Cora listed off most of the cafes they'd seen on their earlier explorations, a few places he'd heard mentioned by others or in reports on the fair, and the upscale dining room at the Inside Inn he'd never actually tried in all his time there.

"The Tyrolean Alps," he finally told her as they stepped through the fair gates. He waved a hand to his right, at the manufactured mountains rising above them.

"German food. Fun! Though I'm not sure I'm dressed for beer."

Adam grinned. "Oh, there are much fancier drinks than beer at this restaurant. Trust me."

"Hmm."

Like proper tourists, they goggled appreciatively at the elaborate recreation of alpine terrain as they entered the exhibit. Slant-roofed buildings welcomed visitors, and a mountain tram carried passengers through the landscape, while the scents of freshly-cooked food wafted out to the hungry crowd.

Adam led Cora past the bustling outdoor cafe and into one of the largest buildings in the area. She staggered to a halt just inside the doors. Before them, rows of neatly arranged tables lined the massive dining hall. Tall arc lights and glittering chandeliers illuminated the space, displaying a high, curved ceiling, faux-marble columns with ornately carved capitals, and elaborately painted trim. Two large murals decorated the center of the ceiling, while smaller images depicting classical and musical themes lined the upper walls. At the far end of the room, a curved apse held a raised stage upon which sat a full orchestra. The sounds of vibrating strings filled the space, punctuated by the low tremors of kettledrums.

"What—" Cora gasped.

Adam grinned sheepishly. "I know you love music."

"This is amazing," she breathed. A moment later she snapped out of her rapture. "And you must be mad. This must cost a fortune!"

Before she could argue further, one of the waitstaff appeared to lead them to a table. He placed them in the center of the room, the perfect location to see all the venue had to offer. Cora's dress shone beneath the lights, while the orchestral sounds swelled around them. She was gorgeous. The expense was worth every penny.

"Do you like it?" Adam asked.

"I love it. But the cost makes me twitch." She flattened her menu on the table, scanning it, her eyes growing wide. "It's worse than I thought! There's a salad for sixty cents!"

Adam shrugged. He didn't usually spend this much on food, but he'd been to pricy business dinners before. Entrees in the multiple dollars wouldn't surprise him.

"Twenty cents for mashed potatoes?" Cora continued. "We could buy two hot dogs for that."

Adam pointed at a spot on the menu. "Imported Frankfurter Sausage. Fifty cents. There's your hot dog."

She scowled at him. "I am not paying fifty cents for a hot dog. I'd like the schnitzel, but it's a whole dollar."

"Order it. Pretend I'm a millionaire. Someday when I'm a famous inventor, you'll look back on this and laugh. Besides, my food will cost even more. I'm going to have…"

He glanced down the menu for something that looked exceptional. If he was going to spend the money he wanted to have the best.

"The calf's brain, obviously." Cora smirked. "Oh, no, wait. That's only sixty cents. You'll have to eat two."

"Actually, I think I want this German dish with the bratwurst and whatever *Wurzeln* and *Kartoffeln* are."

"Root vegetables and potatoes," Cora translated.

"You speak German?"

"Oh, fluently." She couldn't suppress a chuckle. "No, not at all, actually. But I think that man over there is eating it." She made a discreet pointing motion.

"Ah. That looks excellent. And I want the mixed pickles to go with it. Which makes my meal one dollar five. Before dessert, of course. Would you be interested in sharing a few things? I'm not sure whether I want the hazelnut torte, the cheesecake, or the *Kirschenkuchen*."

"We'll never be able to eat all that."

"Then we'll take it home with us. Eat it later in the hotel. Or for breakfast in the morning. Spare no expense. This is your Olympic celebration meal."

"I haven't even won anything."

You've won my heart. That's enough.

Adam's fingers twitched. He wanted to reach across the table and cover her hand with his own. Pour out his heart to her. Beg her to be his.

"*Guten Abend, meine Dame, mein Herr,*" a helpful waiter interrupted before Adam could lose all good sense and say something he'd regret. "What can I get for you this evening?"

Adam ordered everything, including the three desserts and a bottle of wine. The whole meal together would total almost four dollars. Enough for a nice pair of boots. Enough for a few replacement tools for work. Maybe he *was* a little crazy to be doing this.

With the music playing, the electric lights shining, and

Cora in front of him, however, it was difficult to consider this outing anything but a smashing success. When the wine was placed before him, he lifted his glass to her.

"Here's to a spectacular, once-in-a-lifetime treat with the most ravishing companion I could imagine. Thank you, Cora, for your friendship, and for agreeing to join me tonight."

She clinked her glass against his, her smile warm and a little shy. "You're welcome."

The wine soon relaxed them both, and they fell into an easy conversation about music that carried them through most of dinner. The food was as fine as he had hoped, and before he knew it, his belly was full and he had three boxed up desserts, ready to take to the hotel for late-night snacking.

Cora sipped the last of her wine and beamed at him. She reached a hand across the table and Adam grasped it. He'd had just enough to drink to blunt any worries about touching her or taking things too far. His thumb skimmed over the back of her hand, rubbing slow, gentle circles.

Under the chandelier's glow, her green eyes resembled liquid pools. Her lips, a rosy pink, had parted slightly. Adam remembered the taste of those lips. Sliding his tongue between them. Urging her into a deep, luxurious kiss.

"Cora," he murmured, "your 'friends plus kissing' idea seems better and better by the moment."

She leaned toward him, despite the table keeping them apart. His grip on her hand tightened.

"I'm glad you think so." Her voice was low and husky. She felt this. As powerfully as he did, perhaps.

"I haven't the stomach for these desserts just now, but what do you say to returning to our room and indulging in a small sampling of some of your potential perquisites?"

Her chest rose and fell in a deep breath, pressing her breasts against the tight fabric of her dress. Adam swallowed hard.

"That sounds delicious," she whispered.

Heat coursed through his body. He squirmed in his seat,

trying to prevent himself from becoming uncomfortably aroused in a public place. He lifted her hand to his lips, pressing a lingering kiss to her knuckles. If they'd had any semblance of privacy, he would be swinging his chair around to sit beside her and hauling her into his arms this very moment.

He rasped her name again. "Cora, I—"

With a sudden zap of electrical energy, the entire room went dark.

14

Excerpt of a letter from Miss Cora Maxwell to Mr. Adam Levett, dated March, 30, 1904

I have been interviewed by the local paper about my training for the Olympic Games! I feel like a star. I've enclosed clippings of the article for you to read at your leisure.

Sept. 7, evening

THE MUSIC STAGGERED TO A HALT. Gasps of shock reverberated from the high ceilings, followed quickly by cries of alarm and confusion. Holding tightly to Adam's hand, Cora pushed her chair back and made her way around the table. He caught her by the waist, pulling her close. Whatever was happening, they wouldn't be separated.

"I've got you." Levett's voice was a soothing murmur. "I won't let anything happen to you."

"That's very sweet of you." Cora ran her hand over the tabletop until she found a fork. Not the best of weapons, but good enough to surprise an attacker in the dark. "But I'm not afraid of a bit of darkness."

"Oh."

Was he disappointed? She supposed it couldn't be easy for a bookish man to feel he was protecting a woman the way the world told him he ought to do. Especially when the woman in question habitually practiced with a lethal weapon.

"Then why are you in my lap?" he asked.

She wasn't. Quite. She was still standing. Directly between his legs. The sudden awareness of his thighs against hers sent a hot pulse of arousal straight to her core. An urge to lean forward tugged at her. Would he be hard like he'd been last night when they were kissing?

Cora curled her fingers more tightly around the fork to keep herself grounded in reality. She couldn't use the darkness for amorous explorations. Not when danger was a real possibility.

The metallic clicks of moving machinery cut through the general clamor, and she whirled automatically toward the nearest sound.

"What's that?"

Adam gave her waist a reassuring squeeze. "The fans. They rotate periodically to provide optimal air circulation. Didn't you notice them during dinner?"

Not an attack, then. Her body relaxed slightly, but she remained standing, improvised weapon in hand. The sound could still be used as cover for mischief.

"That means electricity is still running to the room. It's only the lights that have been tampered with."

"It could be accidental," Levett argued. "A place this big, things are bound to go wrong now and again."

Cora sniffed. Hadn't he been marveling the other day about her positivity? Clearly, he was at least as optimistic as she was.

She scanned the room. Here and there spots of light appeared as people lit matches. The fearful chattering continued to rise in volume.

"Ladies and gentlemen!" a voice boomed. The din of voices slowly subsided to a low rumble. "Please remain in your seats.

There is no cause for panic. We have experienced a slight malfunction, but are working on the problem as I speak. The lights will be restored soon. Again, for your own safety, please remain in your seats. Thank you."

"I don't like this," Cora muttered. Around her the voices of other patrons rose again, perhaps expressing similar sentiments.

"If someone meant us harm, there are many better ways to go about it than an attack in a crowded dining hall," Adam pointed out.

"True. But perhaps physical harm isn't the goal. I find it difficult to believe we repeatedly happen to stumble upon mechanical malfunctions."

"It does rouse suspicion," he agreed. His voice remained soothing, but his grip on her had yet to loosen. He wasn't as calm as he pretended.

Overhead, a single chandelier winked to life. Then another. Cheers rose from the crowd. Soon, lights all across the room were glowing yellow-white, restoring the chamber to full illumination. On stage, the musicians lifted their instruments and began to play as if the interruption had never happened.

Cora dropped her fork on the table and stepped from Levett's grasp before anyone could berate her for impropriety. Though she suspected more than one couple had used the situation as an excuse for comforting one another. She picked up the boxes of desserts.

"Let's get out of here."

"Yes, let's." Adam poured the last of the wine into his glass and drained the entire thing in one gulp. Definitely not as calm as he'd been acting. He waved a hand to catch the attention of the nearest waiter. How many of the staff had been caught standing with food in their hands when the lights went out? The fact that disastrous spills hadn't happened all over was quite remarkable.

Adam paid the exorbitant dinner bill with several crisply folded dollars. He'd probably had them stashed carefully away until this evening. Cora still wanted to scold him for insisting upon this expense, but she couldn't stop the flutter in her belly thinking how ardently he'd campaigned for this outing with her.

Was she falling for him? Or was it a passing infatuation mingling with their friendship? How on earth did one make any sense of all these emotions? Relationships were nothing if not confusing.

She jogged to keep pace with Adam's long strides as they left the restaurant, holding up her skirts to protect her dress. It really was beautiful, and she was glad Adam liked it. She'd brought it in case she decided upon a celebratory dinner when the Olympic Games finished. Now she was doubly glad of the decision.

"Excuse me, sir," a voice called out. A pale man with a receding hairline jumped into Cora and Adam's path, forcing them to halt. "My name is Roger Franklin, and I'm covering the Exposition for the St. Louis Post-Dispatch. I understand there was an electrical malfunction inside the Luchow-Faust restaurant this evening?"

"Er, yes," Levett replied.

"You were inside? Could you tell me something of your experience?"

"The lights went out."

"Ah. And what was that like?"

"Dark."

Cora winced. Levett made a poor interview candidate. He was much too matter-of-fact.

"Was there any trouble? Commotion? Panic?"

"People were chattering. I'm sure some were afraid. But no real trouble. It was quickly resolved."

"And what was the problem?"

"A malfunction, was all they said. If I had to guess, I'd say a short in a wire or an issue with the master switch. Easily fixed. Not even worth a mention in your paper, I'm afraid."

Levett shifted in agitation. He wanted to leave, but was too polite to simply walk away.

"Do you think this incident might have been deliberate sabotage?" the reporter pressed.

"Uh…"

Cora grasped Levett's arm firmly. "Adam, darling, my headache is growing quite unbearable. Perhaps we might hurry home?"

"Oh, er, yes. Of course. Please excuse us."

The reporter nodded and stepped away. "I'll leave you to see to your wife's health. Might I get your name before you go?"

"Uh, Levett. Adam Levett." He gave the man a quick departing nod and hurried on, taking Cora's arm as if she truly needed assistance.

"You shouldn't have given him your name," Cora hissed.

"Why?"

"It just seems suspicious that he picked us out of the departing crowd. Directly after a suspicious occurrence." She tucked the boxes of desserts more securely under her free arm. "Let's go home and eat these away from all this chaos. I'm tired of people. I'd prefer some quiet time with just the two of us."

Adam's mouth turned up in a thoughtful smile. "Quiet. Just us. Sounds delightful."

15

Excerpt of a letter from Mr. Adam Levett to Miss Cora Maxwell, dated June 27, 1904—unsent

My dear Miss Maxwell. As I prepare to leave for St. Louis, I feel I must confess something to you. Over the course of this correspondence, I have begun to develop an affection for you that, while neither superior to nor deeper than our friendship, is, I fear, profoundly different.

CORA DRUMMED HER FINGERS on the table—the desk, rather—that Adam had dragged across the room to allow her to use the bed as a makeshift chair.

"We have a problem," she declared.

Adam nodded. One problem? He could think of many problems, starting with the fact that she was sitting only the width of the desk away from him, clad in nothing but her nightgown. Then there was the matter of their interrupted dinner. Just when he'd settled on an evening of kissing, the lights had gone out. Now he was second-guessing his decision. He and Cora hadn't touched since boarding the trolley back to the hotel.

More accurately, he hadn't dared touch her. He couldn't let anything go too far. He didn't habitually carry contraceptives, and it wasn't as if there were hawkers at the fair selling them. As far as he knew. If anything were to happen tonight, it needed to be entirely controlled and rational. Which was the exact opposite of the emotions she stirred in him.

"What's the problem?" he asked. Might as well add hers to the list.

"We don't have a knife." She gestured at the three pieces of cake sitting between them. "You may have to stand with the cake on your head while I shoot it down the middle with an arrow."

"Ah." He grinned, some of the tension leaching from his body. This was Cora. He could relax around her. He only needed to remember that. "Sounds a bit messy."

"Not at all. I'll lay down a sheet first to catch the blood."

"Hah. You shoot better than that."

Cora's eyebrows twitched. "Oh, it won't be my fault. It'll be yours. You fidget. I can feel your leg jiggling right now. It's vibrating the table."

Adam froze. "Sorry."

"It's not a problem," she added quickly. "Simply one of those quirks you have. It's fun, learning things I could never discover through letters no matter how many you write me."

"I agree." He'd already picked up on so many things about her. Like the big freckle on the left side of her nose. Or her purposeful strides that could almost match his habitually rapid pace. The way her body became absolutely still when she focused. The way it melted against him when he kissed her.

"I have a better solution to your cake problem," he said. "One that also addresses the fact that we have no forks."

"Oh?"

He picked up the slice of cheesecake and lifted it to her lips. "Have a bite."

She did, chewing slowly before licking her lips. Every nerve in Adam's body jolted awake.

"Delicious." She picked up the hazelnut torte. "You try this one."

Adam sampled a small bite of the rich chocolate cake, letting it linger on his tongue, watching Cora's mouth the entire time. Her lips were fractionally apart, and she stared at him as he ate. Was she thinking about kissing him? Because he was absolutely thinking about kissing her.

"How was it?" she asked.

"Almost perfect."

"Almost?" Her nose scrunched as she frowned at him. She set down the slice of cake. Smears of chocolate hazelnut cream coated her fingers.

Adam's hand shot out to catch her wrist before she could lick the icing away herself. Already he was losing control. And already he didn't care. He raised her hand to his mouth.

"This bite will be perfect," he murmured.

He was right. The chocolate on her fingers tasted divine. Her sharp gasp of breath as he stroked his tongue across her skin set his blood to boiling.

"*Mmm.* Yes. Perfect." He released her hand and rose from his seat, dragging the desk away from the bed. "But I think I'm done with dessert for now."

Just a taste. Just a taste of cake. Just a taste of Cora.

Cora stared up at him, scooting to the very edge of the bed. Her nightgown caught beneath her, sliding up her calves as she moved. "But what if I'm not done?"

The breathy quality of her voice spurred him on. He scooped up a glob of chocolate with one finger. "Try this."

Adam walked to her side and pressed the finger to her lips. Her tongue snaked out, probing, then she wrapped her lips around his finger and sucked every drop of cake away. Lord, what a mouth. He wanted it all over his body. He'd already stripped off his jacket and vest, but even his shirt was too hot.

Her gaze dropped to his groin and his cock swelled impossibly harder.

"Do you like what you do to me?" he rasped.

"Yes."

"Good." He let the finger she'd just licked trail over the buttons along the front of her nightgown. "Your beautiful breasts were on display all evening, and now you've covered them up. I will have to remedy that."

Adam unfastened the top button. Cora let out a long, slow breath, exactly as she did when preparing to shoot. But here there was no target. Here, her focus was him, and her cupid's bolts struck swiftly and stuck fast.

Adam moved to the second button. "I'm going to kiss you." With the third button, his finger grazed the smooth slope of one breast. "First on the mouth. Then lower. Down here."

This time, he made his caress longer, more deliberate. The nightgown had begun to slip from her shoulders.

"I'll kiss your breasts. Tease your nipples with my tongue and suck them. And when you're trembling, I'll keep going down, down, until my breath is on your thighs and I can kiss and lick your sex until you're sobbing with pleasure."

Adam released the last of the buttons. Cora made a small shimmy and the nightgown fell away to her waist. He took his time enjoying the sight of her, taking in the toned muscles of her arms and abdomen. The skin her evening dress had hidden was a paler color than that above, which was paler still than her tanned arms.

"I'm going to kiss all the places even the sun can't," he vowed. "Now lie back on the bed."

Cora did as she was told, sliding out of the nightgown as she did so, leaving her clad only in a short pair of pale pink satin drawers. "You are uncommonly bossy in the bedroom," she remarked.

Adam climbed onto the bed, straddling her thighs and grinning down at her. "And you're uncommonly obedient."

"Not at all. As an athlete, I understand the importance of following the rules."

Adam cupped her breasts, kneading gently, loving their softness and the way she sighed at his touch. "This is *not* following the rules." He rubbed a thumb over one reddish-brown nipple, bringing it to a taut peak. "This is breaking many, many of them."

"I never said *whose* rules I was following. Maybe I like yours better than theirs."

The way her eyes closed and her mouth gaped as he stroked her said she absolutely did. He bent to taste her lips, his fingers continuing their thorough perusal of her body. She met his kiss with a desperate hunger, giving and taking in equal measure. She groaned when his lips trailed over her jaw and down her throat.

"You taste much better than dessert," he whispered.

As promised, he kissed his way to her breasts, lavishing attention first on one nipple, then the other. Her body arched into him, small, helpless mewls of pleasure escaping her throat. He trailed his hands down over her pretty underpants.

"These are fancy," he remarked. "Did you wear them just for me?"

"No." The word was breathless. "They're all like that. I enjoy looking pretty, even just for me."

"*Mmm.*" Adam pressed a kiss right over her navel. "Pretty and sensible. An intoxicating combination. And right now, definitely not just for you. A gift for me." He untied the string of her drawers and tugged them down, exposing the reddish-brown curls guarding her sex. "Eager to be unwrapped." He slid one hand between her legs, finding her drenched with arousal. "Very, very eager."

"Yes," she gasped. He slid a finger inside her. "More."

Adam kissed his way along her thigh, sliding a second finger into her. She lifted her hips to take him deeper. God, she was lusty. Her arousal made him ravenous with desire. For a long time now he'd had only himself and his imaginings of doing these very things to her. Now he was living the dream and he wanted to savor every second of it.

His tongue circled her clitoris, drawing a blissful moan from her. He repeated the movement, pumping his fingers in and out of her as he worked her swollen bud.

"Adam," she sighed. "This is... better. Better than I... imagined."

Blood pounded in his veins. Had she fantasized about him? Had she touched herself thinking about him? That erotic mental image was so powerful he had to reach down and free his cock from his trousers. His fingers clenched around it, stroking himself as he sucked and licked at Cora's clit.

God, yes.

Her hips bucked. She gasped again and tried to say something, but the words were choked off beneath her groan of need. Adam flicked, teased, sucked, moving his fingers in and out of her in the same rapid rhythm he was using to pleasure himself.

Cora broke with a cry, trembling beneath him in a magnificent orgasm. Adam slowly pulled away, sitting up to observe the aftermath of her climax. Her skin was flushed a glorious pink, and the soft mounds of her breasts rose and fell with each deep breath. Her eyes were alight with pleasure, and a small, dreamy smile curved her rosy lips.

"Cora," he moaned. "Goddamn."

Her gaze focused on him once again, her eyes widening when she realized what he was doing.

"Would you like me to—"

Adam pumped harder, the orgasm building deep inside him. "I just want to look at you."

So many times. So many times he'd imagined seeing her like this, naked and sated at his hands. Never believing he'd see it. The reality of it was beyond glorious. Beyond anything.

He growled her name, taking himself over the edge with a few swift strokes, spending across her belly. Marking her as his.

Mine. You are all mine.

He had no idea how he would manage that outside the bedroom, where he was absent-minded, unemployed Mr. Levett and she was independent, doesn't-need-anyone Cora. Tonight, though, he had her exactly where he wanted her. He rolled onto his back and pulled her close.

"I officially approve of 'friends with kissing,'" he declared. "Though I think we may have gone far enough to consider it 'friends with fucking.' I'll leave you to decide which term suits best."

Cora looked at him with eyes wide. "Are you going to… fuck me? All the way?"

"Tonight? No. Sometime in the future? If you are amenable?"

She nodded vigorously.

Adam's hands tightened possessively around her. "Absolutely."

16

Excerpt of a letter from Miss Cora Maxwell to Mr. Adam Levett, dated May 1, 1904

Mr. Benedict Howard has come courting <u>again</u>. I should feel something romantic for him. I know I should. He is the right age, well-situated, and not unpleasant to look upon. But I feel nothing. Do you know anything about romance, Mr. Levett? Because I can't make sense of it.

CORA DASHED DOWN THE HALL, clutching her still-unbuttoned nightgown. A sleepy haze fogged her mind, and her legs weren't yet steady after that blistering climax. A quick trip to the washroom had allowed her to relieve herself and wash up more thoroughly than the few, quick swipes of Adam's handkerchief. Now, her bed called. She hurried, afraid she'd been away long enough for him to recover from his own orgasm and abandon her bed for his own.

Cora didn't want to sleep alone. She wanted to curl up against his chest, listen to the beating of his heart, feel his arms gathering her close. She wanted him to warm her if she grew cold, and wake her in the morning with a gentle kiss.

She slipped into her room, locking the door behind her. Adam had turned down the lights while she'd been gone, leaving only a single lamp at her bedside. The desk was restored to its proper location, the cakes in their boxes laid neatly on the windowsill, where the cool breeze would help keep them fresh until morning. Adam had undressed, hung his clothes, and changed into a plain white nightshirt.

"Ready to turn in?" he asked, from his seat at the foot of her bed. Her bed. Not his.

Eagerly, Cora rushed into his arms, squirming between the sheets with him and snuggling into his embrace. With their bodies twined, she gave herself over to the sleepiness their amorous exploits had caused. He would hold her. He would warm her. He would...

He didn't wake her with a kiss.

She wasn't honestly sure whether she'd woken first or he had. They'd come unwound from one another in the night, no longer embracing, but still touching. Neither moved. Neither spoke. Sunlight poured through the window, warming Cora's skin where her arm stuck out from beneath the blankets.

Awkward minutes ticked by. Should she hug him? Kiss him? Say something? Surely there were rules or conventions for what one did after a night of passion. She'd expected something romantic. *"My darling." He would shower her with abandoned kisses as he said this. "I never wish to leave your bed again. You are all the food I need. The air I breathe. The—"*

"Good morning," Adam actually said.

"Oh," Cora blurted. "Good morning."

"I hope you slept well." He still hadn't moved. His leg was pressed against hers, skin to skin, her nightgown hiked up past her knees. And yet somehow, he was talking as casually as if he were in the other bed, fully dressed, with no thoughts of kissing in his head whatsoever.

"Yes. Thank you." The calm in her own voice surprised her.

His proximity had her body raging with desire, yet here they were, exchanging friendly morning greetings.

They were friends, after all. Even if they were friends with...

Her cheeks flamed. She could hardly even think that word in the daylight. Inside, though, she yearned to hear him say it again. In that low, seductive voice that commanded her to climb into bed and do wicked things with him.

"We should rise and prepare for the day," Adam said. Was there uncertainty in his voice? Probably she was imagining it. "I'm sure you have practicing to do."

"No shooting today. Strength exercises. Then walking. It was meant to be a day exploring the fair."

"Ah, of course. I'll, uh, let you dress." He rolled out of bed, grabbed up some clothing, and hurried from the room.

Cora stared after him. One thing was clear. There would be no kissing this morning.

She shoved herself out of bed and dressed, slowly enough that her hair was still down when Adam returned. She yanked it back into a simple ponytail and accepted the fork he had fetched so they could eat their cake in a civilized, non-sexual fashion.

Disappointing. The desserts didn't taste nearly as good as they had last night. Cora gobbled down her breakfast and started on her exercises for the day.

Throughout her training regimen, Adam sat at the desk and worked on his inventions. They talked little. They kissed not at all. It was unexceptionally normal. Why did that leave a knot of dismay in her gut? Surely he would kiss her again tonight. What more did she want?

Everything.

The memories of his touch played in her head like a moving picture. Yes, she wanted more of that. She wanted the smoldering looks he'd given her across the dinner table. The tiny brushes of his fingers over hers. Hoarse whispers of her name. Moans of desire and pleasure.

What would it take to satisfy these cravings inside her? And why was she yearning for just a tiny kiss or brief moment in his arms? Even the gentle squeeze of his hand. She hadn't expected her perquisites would lead to such strong—and confusing—emotions.

Live and learn.

The weather today was exquisite: a sunny blue sky dotted with puffy white clouds, the temperature warm but not stifling. The gorgeous day must have tempted all the locals out to the fair, because the crowd was the largest Cora had ever seen.

She walked at Adam's side in their usual close-but-not-touching way. Perhaps given the number of people here, it would be better to take his arm. Or even hold his hand. After all, she didn't want to become separated. The possibility remained that someone wished him harm.

Surveying the crowd for any suspicious persons, Cora caught sight of a pair of young lovers, leaning against the rail along the Grand Basin. The man whispered something in the woman's ear and she smiled, her face alight with happiness.

A pang of jealousy stabbed at Cora's chest. Why couldn't she have that? She'd always been a romantic. But a hopeful romantic, certain that someday she'd experience a magic *zing* when she met The One. So far, no knight for this well-armed damsel.

She'd learned one thing for certain, though. She would never marry Benedict Howard. Nor any man who didn't make her body wild the way Adam did. Cora Maxwell would never settle for a boring marriage bed.

"Flowers for your lady?" a hawker called.

Cora jumped. Was he talking to them?

But, no. A tall, black-haired gentleman was pulling out a coin to buy a flower for his lovely wife. A bouncing little girl in a pink dress stood between them.

Stop being silly, Cora scolded herself. *Can't you behave normally like Adam is doing?*

Maybe the first step was to stop calling him by his given name.

"So, Mr. Levett," she said breezily. "Was there anything in particular you wished to see today?"

Adam—Levett—gave her a look of confusion, then shook his head. "Uh, no, not especially. I was following you."

"Ah."

The conversation died. Neither of them had much talent for making small talk, but today they were more silent than usual. Probably it was her fault. She was lost in her muddled thoughts. Friends with kissing had been her idea in the first place, and now she was the one reacting strangely to it.

"Perhaps the Ferris wheel?" Adam asked after another minute of aimless wandering.

"I'm a bit afraid of a malfunction."

"True, after the strange things we've encountered so far. But dropping a dragon in the water ride and turning off some lights are both relatively simple. Stopping a massive piece of engineering like the Ferris wheel? With so many people in and around it? I think that's an entirely different level of difficulty. I doubt our harasser—if such a person exists—would be up to the task."

"Or you're merely making excuses because you want to ride it."

He grinned and Cora felt an odd flip-flopping sensation in her belly. Not good. She would have expected last night's activities to calm some of her attraction to him. After all, she'd gotten what she wanted. Instead, she wanted him even more and her body had begun to react to every tiny detail about him.

He adjusted his spectacles. She liked the way he did that. She liked the way he never seemed quite still, even when they paused. Oh, dear.

The path to the Ferris wheel was clogged with couples.

Couples strolling arm in arm. Leaning close to whisper private things. Smiling into one another's eyes. With each pair they passed, Cora grew more agitated. She wanted Adam to do these things with her. She ached for it.

He never touched her, though, and she didn't dare touch him. She couldn't disrupt their friendship because her romantic side had come unhinged. Apparently, friends with kissing had been her worst idea ever.

"Step right up, ladies and gentlemen!" shouted a fair worker in a crisp blue uniform shirt with matching cap. "Mr. Ferris's original observation wheel, brought all the way from Chicago! Rising two hundred sixty-four feet in the air and using the best modern steam engine with the power of a thousand horses! Only fifty cents each to see the whole world!"

"Two hundred sixty four feet?" Levett mused. "Hmm. Given the known curvature of the earth… In truth I'd estimate we'll be able to see between fifteen and twenty miles. Hardly the whole world."

Cora giggled. Giggled! Shouldn't she be scolding him for being pedantic instead of thinking that his engineer brain was cute?

Inwardly she groaned.

Adam Levett is not cute.

But he was. He was dreadfully cute and she could sooner command the sun to disappear than stop herself from sighing over him.

"I imagine it feels like seeing the entire world, though," she argued. Maybe if she said enough normal things she could squelch her abnormal feelings.

"I'm sure it does," he agreed. "Emotions and logic seem to be often at odds."

Honest truth. Hers certainly had no rationality. If they did, she wouldn't now be suffering one of her wild infatuations for her best friend. The only good she could see in this was that these feelings usually burned out quickly. She wouldn't have to suffer long.

"Good afternoon, sir, miss," the fair worker greeted them as they approached the ticket booth. "Are you here for the wedding?"

"Wedding?" Cora gaped at the man.

"Car's coming around right now," he said, waving his hand. "All done up with flowers and trimmings for the happy couple. Are you part of the party?"

The wheel finished its next partial rotation, halting with the wedding car in the loading area. Pastel trimmings decorated the train-car-sized compartment, and tinkling piano music floated from inside. A man and a woman in their finest clothes rushed toward it, hand-in-hand, beaming at one another.

Cora spun away. "I don't want to be here right now." She darted off, not looking to see if Adam was following her.

"Cora!" Adam caught up with her in mere seconds. "Cora, are you okay? Is something wrong?"

"I can't ride the Ferris wheel today. I don't want anything to go wrong. I don't want to put all those other people at risk."

I don't want to see weddings and flowers and things that make me think about kissing.

"That's fine," he replied. "Another time. But you seem agitated today. Quiet. Is it... Is it something I've done?"

She shook her head.

"Was it... Do you regret last night?"

"No!" Cora's shout was so sudden and so loud that a number of people turned to stare at them. She lowered her voice. "No, not at all."

Last night had been spectacular. But how did she explain to him that it hadn't eased her desire for him but only increased it? That it had left her wanting to swoon in his arms so he would carry her off to his castle and ravish her.

"I read too many novels," she sighed.

His brow crinkled in confusion. "Adventure stories, you

mean? Is that why you're afraid of someone coming after us? What about this: we'll view only outdoor exhibits today. No machines, no lights. How about sports? What Olympic events are happening today?"

Cora smiled up at him. He was such a genuinely good friend. This was why she had to be sensible. He meant too much to her to be just a man she'd been briefly obsessed with. She couldn't let him become that.

"Fencing. Do you know anything about fencing?"

"It's good for keeping cows from escaping."

Cora gave him a jab with her elbow. This was right. This was normal. "Sword fighting. Sabres and epees."

"Oh, *that* fencing. Nope. Know nothing about it. Will you teach me?"

"It would be my pleasure. Let's go."

They jogged the mile to the athletic field, where they slipped into a pair of seats in the back to watch the event already in progress.

"Hit!" declared the judge. "Point Mr. Fonst."

A small cluster of fans seated in the front cheered the Cuban athlete, and he acknowledged them with a tiny lift of his sword. The competitors took up their positions, and the judge signaled for them to begin again.

It quickly became clear to Cora that Mr. Fonst was by far the best swordsman. He dispatched his opponent with ease, then moved on to the next, defeating him with equal precision. By the end of the semifinal round, only one opponent, an American named Van Zo Post, had given him any challenge. Fonst's fans continued to cheer, and Cora finally—finally!—began to relax.

"I have another idea," Adam chattered enthusiastically as the competitors took their break before the final round. "Electrified clothing!"

"What?" Cora frowned at him. "That sounds awful."

"No, no. For scoring. You add wires to the protective

clothing that the fencers wear. In all the locations where a hit should count for a point. You also electrify the sword. If the sword touches in a scoring location, it will trigger a 'hit' signal. If it touches anywhere else, it triggers a 'no-hit' signal."

"And how do the fencers not get electrocuted from their swords?"

"Oh, well, it doesn't need to be large or dangerous amounts of electricity. Like the Electro-Flex. The wires won't be directly touching a person." He pulled out his notebook and began to scribble. "This is brilliant, Cora. Our sports technology business is going to be phenomenal."

Our business. A shiver of delight trembled through Cora that had nothing to do with kisses or infatuations. Adam believed one hundred percent in this vision of the future. Exactly like her visions of winning Olympic gold. He meant to realize this dream, and he meant to include her in it. She *could not* mess this up.

The fencing began again, and Cora focused her attention on watching Fonst and Van Zo Post rout their competitors. The gold and silver medals would belong to those two for certain. Adam mumbled things about electricity and numbers, fortunately not expecting Cora to know what he was talking about.

"Sense-o-Touch electronic scoring system," she said. He jotted it down. "Just an idea. Could also be something about 'resist' or 'point.'"

"Uh-huh." He made more notes, the match continuing in the background.

"Watch now," Cora instructed, when the top two competitors took their places for the final bout. "These two are clearly the best and you should pay attention. I think Mr. Fonst will win again. Look how focused he is. And how perfect his stance is. He knows he's going to win."

Adam glanced up from his notes to view the competition.

"Like you," he murmured. "You look like that when you shoot. So confident. So determined."

His voice had a husky quality to it, and Cora struggled against the urge to scoot closer. Heat washed over her skin. Her lips tingled, remembering his kiss.

No, no, no. This was not the time or place. Not when she'd just settled into a comfortable state of mind. She stared at the fencers, refusing to even glance at Adam.

Fonst took the lead early and maintained it throughout, though Van Zo Post put in a good effort. The cheers of the Fonst fan club grew increasingly energetic with each point scored, and when the judge called the match, they leapt from their seats, whooping and hugging one another. A few fans tossed bouquets of flowers to Fonst, which he scooped up with a bow and a sweep of his sword.

"I'm glad he has friends and family here to see him," Adam remarked. "That must make it all the more special." Fonst plucked a single red rose from a bouquet and walked over to the crowd, presenting it to a woman in the very front row. Adam's voice dropped back into that husky murmur. "And a sweetheart, apparently."

Cora's gut knotted. Here too? Could she never get away from romance? She stood up abruptly. "Excuse me. I should be going. I have some things to do. Alone. Exercise. And, uh, phone calls. Letters to write. Excuse me."

She dashed from the stands before Levett could say another word. She'd leave the fair. Walk around town, perhaps. Eat dinner on her own. Anything to take her mind off him.

It wasn't until the Intramural train had pulled away from the station that she realized: she'd left Adam all alone. With possible enemies out to harm him.

17

Excerpt of a letter from Mr. Adam Levett to Miss Cora Maxwell, dated May 4, 1904

You asked me in your previous letter whether I knew anything about romance. While I do know the traditional customs of courtship, I do not believe myself a suitable candidate to advise you on the subject.

Sept. 8, late afternoon

"Welcome to AutomaTech. The leader in—"

"Dash it all, Doyle, can't you turn that thing off?" Adam called over the recorded voice.

Doyle glanced up from his newspaper. "And get my ass fired too? No, thanks. What are you doing here? Shouldn't you be off romancing your archer?"

Adam leaned on a display shelf, no longer caring if he knocked anything down. "I think I've ruined everything."

Doyle sighed, folded the newspaper, and set it aside. "Why? What did you do?"

Adam glanced around the room. The exhibit wasn't getting much traffic, if Doyle was spending his time sitting on the rickety stool with his nose in his paper, but Adam wouldn't talk about Cora with tourists in earshot. Several people were passing by along the hall, but none seemed inclined to pass through the AutomaTech gate. The pedestal where the Electro-Flex had once sat now held an electric spaghetti fork. It was one of the worst sellers in the entire catalog.

"I don't know," he whispered, moving closer to Doyle just in case anyone approached. "I think she was enjoying her time with me, despite the odd happenings, and we had a lovely dinner last night, but since we woke up this morning—"

"Oh my God, you slept with her."

Adam's head swiveled around, checking again for anyone watching or listening. "For God's sake, keep your voice down."

"You did! Damnation." Doyle ran a hand through his blond hair. "I hope you were careful."

"Would you shut up?" Adam hissed. "I didn't. Quite. Sort of."

Doyle rolled his eyes skyward. "All right, then. What *did* you do?"

"We messed around a bit," he whispered. "Spent the night in the same bed. But nothing with… consequences."

Doyle snorted. "You mean you didn't stick your cock in her and you won't be a daddy nine months from now. But sounds to me like there were still consequences."

Adam wasn't sure what he wanted more: to punch Doyle in the mouth or to bang his own head against the wall. "Shut. Up. We are in public."

"You started the conversation."

Adam glanced around the empty exhibit once more. "Please. I need help. Tell me what to do."

"Buy some condoms."

"Where? It's not like they're available for sale at the corner drug store. I wouldn't even know where to ask in this city. Besides, that's not the point. Cora was acting peculiar.

Avoiding me, I think. I think I upset her, but I don't know how. I swear I did my best to be my usual self."

Doyle's eyebrows rose. "And does your usual self shower her with kisses and flowers and compliments?"

One side of Adam's mouth scrunched up in a grimace. "No, of course not. We're friends. That's not typical friend behavior."

"Neither is hopping into bed together." Doyle put his face in his hands. "Christ, Adam."

"She hates me. I pushed her too far and now she feels I've dishonored her. That's it, isn't it?"

"More likely she's angry that you didn't buy her flowers and tell her how much you adore her."

"She wanted to be *friends*."

Doyle only shook his head. "Look—" He jerked upright. "Shit. That's Rawley headed this way. Get going before he sees you and reports it to Hampton. If you need to talk more, come back tomorrow. After lunch. Rawley's got the morning shift. Now go."

"But—"

"Buy her flowers. Go."

Adam scampered out the back of the exhibit. The last thing he needed was to get Doyle in trouble on top of everything else. He took the long way around the pentagonal building, wandering slowly past booth after booth, mulling over his problems. He did want to woo Cora. But he also wanted to be her friend, and he didn't want to pressure her if that's all she wanted. Had he been too cuddly last night? Maybe he ought to have slept in his own bed. He'd thought she'd been happy to snuggle.

"Magic flowers! Buy one for your mother! Give one to your lady friend!"

Adam paused, surveying the wares at the small booth. An assortment of small, brass flowers lined the stall. He picked one up to examine it. When his hand closed around the stem, the petals unfolded to reveal a tiny silver bee, buzzing softly in the center of the flower.

"Brilliant!"

The salesman grinned. "Ain't it, though?"

"Battery powered?"

"'Tis. Two fifty and it's yours."

"One fifty." Adam didn't know if he was supposed to barter, but it was worth a try. He'd already blown quite a bit of money on last night's dinner. He dug the coins out of his pocket that he'd meant to spend on the Ferris wheel and began to count them out.

"Two twenty-five," the salesman said.

Adam continued counting out coins. "One seventy-five, one eighty-five, one ninety, one ninety-five. That's all I've got."

"Good enough," the salesman sighed, though he probably could easily have parted with the flower for one fifty. Adam didn't care. He had a gift for Cora. Whatever the trouble, he would at least be able to show her that he meant to make it up to her.

"Cleaning rats for home and office!" proclaimed one of the omni-present salespeople.

Adam stepped to one side to avoid trampling the little machines as they darted about.

"Tagget original design!" the salesman continued. "Would you like to see one in action?"

Adam kept his gaze fixed firmly on the exit door. "Thank you, but—" A cry and the clatter of metal against the wooden floor made him freeze in his tracks. That was too loud for a cleaning rat. He whirled toward the sound.

A canine dragon came barreling directly at him, a long chain trailing behind. Somewhere in the distance, its owner shouted for it to stop.

Adam darted to the side, quick enough to avoid a collision with the dragon. The dangling chain, however, whipped at his ankles, knocking him off balance. He flailed, grabbing for anything that might keep him upright.

His fingers closed around smooth rubber. An electrical cord. The machine it was attached to tumbled from the display shelf and Adam tumbled backward. Time seemed to slow as his body careened into the shelf. Metal creaked. Electrical mechanisms popped. Pain jolted through him as his body slammed into the floor and an entire exhibit's worth of electrical devices crashed down atop him.

18

Excerpt of a letter from Miss Cora Maxwell to Mr. Adam Levett, dated August 7, 1903

Ouch. In my excitement over my rehabilitation, I pushed a bit too hard the last few days. Thankfully, I have the Electro-Flex on low power and a lovely lavender ointment to ease bruised or aching muscles.

Sept. 8, evening

PRINTED PHOTOGRAPHS AND BOLD headlines pleaded for Cora's attention, but her unsettled mind continued to read the same paragraph over and over, unable to retain the information. She straightened the newspaper, adjusted her position on her bed, and tried yet another article.

A sharp rap on the door interrupted before she could read more than two sentences.

"Cora! Are you in there?"

"Adam!" She flung the paper aside and leapt from the bed, racing to the door to let him in.

Thank God. After an hour of fruitlessly wandering the fair with no idea where he might have gone, she'd given up and returned to the hotel, only to spend the entire afternoon in a state of near panic. She'd left him. For the most ridiculous of reasons.

She yanked the door open. Now he was here and she could finally—

Cora gasped aloud, her hand flying up to cover her mouth. A smear of dried blood matted Adam's hair just above his left temple and a bruise was forming across his cheek. His suit was torn and dirty, stained with what looked to be more blood, and singed in several places along his right side. He wasn't wearing his spectacles, and he squinted at her before slipping past her into the room, limping a little.

"Good God, what happened?" She shoved the door closed and locked it, fighting the urge to shove a chair beneath the handle in case whoever had done this to him hadn't finished the job. "Do you need a doctor? A hospital? Should I call for help? Please, sit down before it gets worse."

Adam chuckled a little and took a seat on the edge of her bed. "I'm fine. I'm sorry I look a mess. Slight mishap. And I might owe my life savings to an electric toaster company. But I'm fine. I promise."

"You are not fine." She assessed him from head to toe, looking for additional signs of injury. It was difficult to gauge the full extent of the damage with his clothes hiding anything beneath. Was he still bleeding? Did he have any broken bones?

"Who did this to you?" she demanded. "Were you attacked?"

"Only by a wall of toast-making machines." He flashed a bashful grin. "It was an accident. I tripped over the leash of someone's pet dragon and crashed into an exhibit. Whole shelf came down. But I'm fine, honest."

"You look awful. Don't move." Cora rushed to the wardrobe, where her small medical kit sat nestled among her possessions. She never traveled without it, in case of cuts, bruises, or other minor injuries that might interfere with her athletic pursuits. "Take off your clothes," she called over her shoulder.

"Planning to ravish me, are you?"

Cora shivered at the seductive timbre of his voice. He couldn't be too badly off if he was thinking about such things, right?

"Take off your clothes and lie back on the bed," she ordered. "No one is doing anything until I've seen to your injuries."

She turned around, medical kit in hand, to find him squirming out of his torn jacket. Good. He set it aside, then did the same with his vest, and finally his shirt.

"The trousers, too," she added. "You were limping and I want to see that leg. You can keep your drawers on if you're feeling shy."

Adam burst into laughter. By the time Cora had fetched a damp cloth from the washstand and carried her supplies to the bed, he was shaking so hard he was holding his side and wincing.

"I don't see what's so funny about this," she grumbled.

"Oh, Lord, Cora." He straightened up and swiped the back of his hand across his eyes. "If you want me naked you can have me naked. You don't need to coax me into it."

"Get out of those trousers, then."

He swiftly removed the last of his clothing, trying to hide his grimaces as he twisted and bent to free his injured leg. When he finished he sprawled on her bed, stark naked and grinning.

"See?" He spread his arms wide. "Undamaged. Fully functional. At your service."

Cora did her best to focus on his injuries and not the contours of his lean body. She shoved his ruined clothes off the bed and sat down beside him.

"Careful," he said. "There's a gift for you in the inside pocket of that coat."

A gift? For me?

"Though maybe I spent the money needlessly, since here I am, in your bed wearing nothing but my birthday suit. I assume that means you don't hate me."

Cora gently wiped the bloody spot at his temple with her cloth. He flinched a bit, but didn't appear in great pain.

"This doesn't look as bad as I feared." She dabbed a bit of ointment on the small wound. "I don't think it needs a bandage."

"Nah," Adam agreed. "Bled like the devil, but since it stopped I've hardly noticed it."

"Good." She swiped the cloth down his cheek, clearing away the last streaks of blood. "Now what else?" Her gaze traveled lower. A few scrapes on his chest, a bruise forming near his left shoulder. "Let me see that right arm. That looks like a burn."

He turned to let her examine the patch of reddened skin. "Some of the toasters were in use."

"This should be bandaged."

"Yes, doctor."

Cora scowled at his teasing tone and set about cleaning the wound and applying ointment. At least he was cheerful. That was a good sign. No broken bones. No serious gashes. She moved on to the right leg, which he'd been favoring when he walked into the room. She did her best to avoid looking at his groin as she climbed over and around him. This was a medical examination, not a seduction.

Unfortunately, the more he smiled and teased and the more she touched him, the harder it was to keep her mind on her task.

"I think you're going to have some bruising here," she said, applying a bit of ointment to his leg and massaging gently. "This should help. It both promotes healing and relieves pain. I've used it many times."

"Smells nice, too." He sighed. "And your hands feel good.

You should definitely rub some on the other leg. And my chest. And take off your clothes and kiss me while you do it."

Cora sat up straight, replaced the cap on her jar of ointment, and wiped her fingers clean. "I'm beginning to wonder if you injured yourself on purpose."

"Nope. But I'll keep it in mind for the future."

She scowled down at him. "Don't you dare."

"Kiss me."

Cora hesitated. If they did this again, would it ease some of her confusion and longing? Or only make it worse? Did she care?

Adam stared at her, his eyes darkened by desire. "Even blurry, you're beautiful," he whispered, his voice low and thick with sensual promise. "Kiss me, Cora. Kiss me everywhere. Kiss me the way I kissed you last night."

No, she didn't care. Right now all she cared about was having her hands on his body and his on her. She dropped her medical kit atop the pile of his clothes and straddled him, claiming his mouth with hers.

His response was merciless, raw, primal. He kissed her deeply, holding nothing back, unafraid to let her feel the full force of his desire. His tongue swept over hers and he sucked on her lips until they felt gloriously swollen. It was intoxicating, the way he shed his mild-tempered disposition and surrendered to his passion. It made her want to join him. To let him sweep her away into a world where nothing existed outside their two bodies.

Cora kissed down his throat, tasting the salt of his skin. Her hands stroked up and down his chest, learning his body, reveling in the forbidden pleasure of touching a man's bare flesh. As she explored, he shoved up her skirts, sliding his hands along her thighs and squeezing her buttocks.

"Silky drawers again," he murmured. "All pretty, just for me." He tugged the undergarment over her hips and she wriggled to help him slide it all the way off. It joined the growing pile on the floor.

His hand delved between her legs, stroking her in that same way that had driven her wild with pleasure last night, teasing her clit with slow, whisper-light circles.

"Adam," she gasped. "Please... would you... lick me again?"

He withdrew his hands and grasped her about the waist. "Certainly, love. And what about you? Would you like to explore me the same way?"

"I think so." She'd read a very salacious story once where a woman had pleasured a man with her mouth, but it hadn't described the act in any detail. She would probably make a hash of it. Which didn't stop her from wanting to try.

"Turn around."

"Um..." Cora let Adam guide her until she was completely upside down atop him, her skirts pushed up past her hips and his mouth so close to her sex that she could feel the warmth of his breath. Beneath her, his erection jutted out, fully hard and within easy kissing distance. Experimentally, she swiped her tongue across the tip.

Adam's groan was magical. "Fuck, yes, love. Just like that. As much as you want."

And then his tongue was on her again, sweeping along her folds, tormenting her clit, and his fingers were inside her, working deep and thrusting hard.

Cora licked and kissed all up and down his shaft, thrilling to his every twitch. When she wrapped her lips around him, he jerked and momentarily faltered in his attentions to her. She didn't even mind.

I'm driving him wild. I'm making him come apart the same way he's doing to me.

It was all so brilliantly wanton. He redoubled his efforts, and she moaned around his cock and rocked her hips against his mouth. At the same time, she sucked him harder, taking him further inside her, clutching at the sheets to anchor herself in this storm of pleasuring and being pleasured.

She was close. She was so close. His tongue found just the right spot, and she cascaded over the edge, gasping and forgetting about what she was supposed to be doing to him as the orgasm swept her away, going on and on until she couldn't take it any longer and she had to reach back and push him away from her too-sensitive flesh.

"Adam," she sighed, then sucked him again, needing to feel him go to pieces the way she had.

"Cora." He thrust upward to meet her downward motions, giving a half-choked moan. Within moments his body was stiffening and shuddering, and a spurt of his hot, bitter seed coated her tongue.

She rolled off him. "Ugh. I think I need a drink of water."

He laughed. An exhausted, satisfied, delighted laugh. "Love, you deserve any sort of drink you desire." He stretched his long limbs and yawned. "Shall I fetch you something? I'd be happy to. And afterward I'd be happy to pleasure you all over again."

Cora climbed out of the bed, adjusting her clothing. "No. You're injured and I'm the one who's still dressed. I'll fetch things. You just... stay there."

He folded his hands behind his head, grinning up at her. "I'll be here. Ready to provide orgasms all night."

Cora's cheeks flamed in response. One would think after what she'd done she'd be a little more sophisticated and a little less awkward. Apparently not. She pulled on a dressing gown over her rumpled dress and stepped into the boots she'd left beside the door, not bothering to tie them.

"Be right back."

She scampered from the room and down the stairs. It was entirely possible that she'd draw some disapproving looks, disheveled as she was, but she did want something to drink, and perhaps a bite to eat as well. She'd been too nervous all afternoon to do more than nibble.

Mostly, though, she wanted a moment away from Adam, to recover from their latest bout of passion. He'd called her "love." More than once. What did that mean? Her heart thudded beneath her breast. Memories of the romantic couples she'd seen throughout the day raced through her mind.

Maybe that can be us.

Not now, though. Not when he'd stumbled into too many "accidents." Not when she had an Olympic competition to prepare for. Those things had to be her focus. And what of their future business together? Could they be friends, lovers, and partners all at once? Partners with Perquisites. Catchy.

So much to think about. But not tonight. Tonight, she was going to have a drink, eat a sandwich, and then ask Adam to make good on that promise of orgasms all night long.

19

Excerpt of a letter from Mr. Adam Levett to Miss Cora Maxwell, dated February 27, 1904

Wouldn't it be fun if I could simply hop into my electric motorcar and drive to Indianapolis to visit you? Perhaps someday when I am famous.

Sept. 12

ADAM BENT THE EARPIECE of his spectacles for what felt like the millionth time in the last several days. He popped them back on. Better? Maybe.

If only his good pair hadn't been crushed in the toaster debacle. This spare pair looked fine, and he could see clearly, but something about them wasn't quite right.

A metaphor for his life, perhaps.

He and Cora had settled into a pattern in the days since his accident. She'd found a local archery club where she could train and spent the better part of every day preparing for her competition. Adam accompanied her, notebook and slide rule in hand, filling page after page with drawings and calculations. Not once had either of them suggested going back to the fair.

It was a comfortable, quiet existence, save for the nights—and perhaps a quick moment in the afternoon—when they pleasured one another to exhaustion with hands and mouths. At times it was blissful, perfect. And yet every day his nagging doubt clawed a little harder. They needed to talk. They needed to agree on what this was and where it was going. Adam had no idea how to broach the subject, much less what to say.

Breakfast had become his favorite time of day, perhaps excepting their sexual exploits. Each morning they sat together in this secluded corner of the hotel restaurant, enjoying a relaxing hour in one another's company before stepping back into the real world. They shared pastries, coffee, and newspapers, and talked of anything and everything unrelated to the World's Fair, his job (or lack thereof), and the Olympics.

Cora, as usual, flipped eagerly through the pages of her newspaper. Not the Post-Dispatch, but some gossipy rag full of sensation and scandal. She loved it. Adam had learned more lurid details about the lives of the rich and famous in the last few days than he'd ever heard in his life. He couldn't care less which tycoon had squandered his money on a 300-foot long airship with Tiffany glass windows or who was sleeping with whom, but he loved Cora's gleeful updates on the most salacious of the stories and her insightful analysis of the likely truths behind the rumors.

Adam looked down at his own paper. He'd been trying to avoid articles about the fair, but today a story about the upcoming motorcar races had sucked him in. The battle of the fuels. Road cars, racing on real streets. Several cars with steam engines would be competing, of course. Adam would be rooting for the battery-powered entry from Baker Electric. And then there was some nonsense about a luxene-powered Mercedes. He'd believe that when he saw it.

"Your first event is on the nineteenth, correct?" he asked. "Will you need to rest afterwards, or do you think we could go and watch—"

Cora gasped in horror.

Adam dropped his paper. "Cora?"

"Oh, no!" She flattened her own paper on the table. Her green eyes were wide, her face pale. "Who would do this?"

"What's wrong?" He reached to take her hand, but she pulled away, instead turning her paper around so he could see it and pointing to a particular article.

"Look. Look what they've done!"

"The Fair's Lord of Chaos," he read. "Sounds a bit over-the-top." His eyes tracked down the page and his heart nearly stopped. "Fucking hell," he gasped.

The Fair's Lord of Chaos

Mad mechanical mishaps follow in the wake of one Mr. Adam Levett of Philadelphia, former AutomaTech employee and eccentric inventor. Dismissed from his position following an altercation that destroyed one of his own creations, Mr. Levett nonetheless continues to roam the grounds of the Louisiana Purchase Exposition, leaving a trail of disasters and electrical malfunctions behind him. Whether encountering rogue dragons that overturn boats, or stumbling into accidents that destroy competitors' exhibits, Mr. Levett appears either unable or unwilling to remain out of trouble.

"A short in a wire or an issue with the master switch," he explained to a reporter after the now-infamous blackout at the exclusive Luchow–Faust restaurant. Mere conjecture on his part, or a sign of more sinister involvement?

"Yes, absolutely," was the resounding answer from AutomaTech employee Robert Doyle, when

asked whether the situation had improved now the company and Mr. Levett had parted ways.

Mr. Levett has also been seen on numerous occasions in the company of a woman who he claimed to be his wife. An investigation by this reporter has determined that Mr. Levett is not and never has been married. We can only conclude that he is involved in an illicit deception with a lady of questionable morals.

Whether Mr. Levett is the perpetrator of disturbances or merely a magnet for unfortunate accidents, we hope for the sake of the general populace he will take his chaos elsewhere and leave the Exposition a safe space for the enjoyment of all.

"I'm going to kill him," Cora snarled. "I'm going to find the anonymous cad who wrote this filthy piece of rubbish and I'm going to put an arrow straight through his rotten heart."

Adam read the article again, his body still frozen in disbelief. He couldn't speak, couldn't rage, couldn't cry.

"How dare they?" Cora continued to seethe. "How dare they do these things to you and then use that against you? Who is it? Who hates you? That boss of yours?"

"Hampton?" Adam pushed the paper away and straightened his shoulders, his mind finally lifting from the fog. "He dislikes me, certainly, but I can't imagine him doing this. He found his excuse to fire me. He can take the Electro-Flex out of his catalog if he likes. From his perspective, he's already won."

"Who else, then? Who would benefit from destroying your reputation?"

Adam shrugged. "No one, as far as I know. Rawley's hated me ever since the flying bicycle crash, but he builds little household things, like hair curlers and auto-dusters and that god-awful electric spaghetti fork. Nothing that would compete with anything I'm planning. I don't even know if anyone besides you even *knows* what I'm planning. Oh, except Doyle."

Cora turned the paper around and scowled at the article for a moment. "That quote of his is suspicious. It could have been an answer to anything. It strikes me as a twisting of words. If he'd deliberately wanted to smear you, wouldn't he have done it outright?"

"It's not him. But he might be able to help. The quote from me must have come from that reporter who accosted us after the power outage at dinner. The same man could have been nosing around the AutomaTech booth, asking questions. Doyle might know something that could help us track him down."

Cora drummed her fingers on the table. "I don't remember that reporter's name, but I suspect it could have been false anyway. He said he was working for the Post-Dispatch and this is certainly not that. Drat. So little to go on. And I'm afraid if we go asking questions, more bad things will start happening."

"Lord of Chaos," Adam mumbled. But the bold headline wasn't what jumped out at him when he looked back down at the article.

Lady of questionable morals.

He rose abruptly. "I have to leave."

"What?" Cora blinked at him.

"This person may have targeted me, but he could destroy both our reputations. I can't stay with you any longer. I must leave before anyone connects me with you and you become the subject of scandal."

Dammit, dammit, dammit. Why had he been so stupid? Had he really thought he could get away with cavorting around with her without anyone finding out?

He didn't need an answer. Truth was, he hadn't cared. He'd wanted her and his selfish desires had kicked all sensible arguments to the curb. He'd put her at risk, just to get under her skirts. The only positive was that he hadn't fully deflowered her. A rather flimsy technicality, in his opinion, but one she could use to her advantage.

"You can't run off on your own with horrible people after you," she protested.

Adam rubbed his temple. "Cora, I must. If your name becomes associated with this, it could end your sporting career. They'll kick you out of the Olympic Games. I can't let that happen."

She glared at him, her jaw clenched, her cheeks hot with fury. Not at him. At the people who had done this to him and the world that would do worse to her.

She pushed her chair back and stood, stepping toward him, blinking back angry tears. "You can't go for me," she ground out. "You need to go for you. Not away from my room, not away from my hotel. Away from everything. Go home. Go further than home. Somewhere new, where no one has heard of you. Where you can build your dream with no one to stop you. Don't sneak back to watch my competition, and don't write me letters. Not until this is long, long over."

Nausea roiled in his gut. She was right. To let this all blow over, to protect her from exposure and shame, he had to sever their connection. And in all likelihood, the separation would become permanent. He gripped the back of his chair to steady himself.

No. Not like this. He'd known, somewhere in the back of his mind, that this wasn't forever. The end of their time at the fair had always loomed. But this sudden, horrid finality stabbed like poison in his belly. She would never be his.

"I'm so sorry, Cora." Somehow the words came out without him either sobbing or collapsing. "I wanted to be there for you. I wanted to be your greatest fan and your loudest supporter."

Her hand shot out to grab his wrist. "You already are. You always will be. Please, go and be safe and well. And when I leave here wearing an Olympic gold medal, I will stand up and shout about your Electro-Flex to every goddamned newspaper in the country." She looked around. At their small corner table behind an overgrown fern, they were mostly shielded from prying eyes. Only someone deliberately watching would be able to see anything of them. Today the rest of the crowd seemed focused on their own matters.

Cora stepped up to him and pressed a long, lingering kiss to his lips. "I will miss your perquisites," she whispered.

"So will I." He would miss everything. Every tiny little thing about her. He'd fallen too deeply to ever escape.

Cora gave him a gentle shove. "Now go. Please. Before anything else happens to you."

Adam stepped reluctantly away from her and started for the exit. The only thing that could hurt him further at this point was if something bad happened to her. He had to go, for her sake. That was clear. But he'd be damned if he left her unprotected.

20

Excerpt of a letter from Miss Cora Maxwell to Mr. Adam Levett, dated May 15, 1904

It's official. I will be traveling to St. Louis in September to compete at the Olympic Games!

Sept. 17

T*HWACK.*

The arrow protruding from the dead center of the target brought Cora a deep satisfaction. She was in top form today. If she shot like this during her events, she wouldn't just win gold. She would destroy her competitors.

Her gaze flicked to the other women practicing here at the athletic field. They seemed like nice people, and it was lovely to meet more women archers. Cora would still happily rout any of them.

"Girl on the end ain't half bad," remarked one of the male archers who leaned against the rail, ogling or snickering, or perhaps watching out of sheer curiosity. "Could give you a run for your money, I wager."

A snort. Cora darted a glance. Thompson.

"She's a haughty bitch," he snarled, probably fully aware she could hear him. "Actually wanted to challenge me in order to show off for some clumsy, bookish fellow, can you believe that? As if she could woo him by performing feats of strength he can't?" Thompson's laugh was spiteful. "What sort of pathetic man would enjoy that?"

Cora's fingers clenched around her bow. *Adam Levett is five thousand times the man you are!* she wanted to scream. But she wouldn't give Thompson the satisfaction of an argument. Especially not when thinking about Adam made her want to weep.

Resisting the urge to reach up and touch the brass flower skewered through her coiffure, she nocked another arrow and let it fly. Another hit in the ten circle. A stray tear trickled from her eye. She was shooting for him and he wouldn't be here to see it.

"Cora!" The masculine voice rang out across the field. "What a beautiful shot! Such a pleasure to see you here at last!"

She whirled around. Benedict! This was unexpected. Still, it was gratifying to be able to prove to Thompson that the world held more than one man who wasn't intimidated by her athletic prowess.

"Oh! Mr. Howard. What a surprise." Cora had to force a smile. Benedict had traveled all this way? Surely that meant he was intending to press his suit. Propose to her, probably. Not what she needed. Between her upcoming competition and the gaping hole left by Adam's departure, she was already under enough stress. She hadn't slept well in days and lack of sleep played havoc with her emotional state.

"Cora!"

A burst of relief flowed through her at the sound of a woman's voice. Thank goodness. Benedict hadn't come alone.

"Jane!" Cora called. Benedict's cousin was one of Cora's dearest friends. Plump and pretty, with a perpetually mischievous smile, Jane never failed to brighten a room.

She sprinted past her cousin on her way to greet Cora. "And Harriet!"

Bringing up the rear, at a far more sedate pace, was Harriet Finch, Jane's neighbor and the third member of their trio. Sober and mathematically-minded, she was surely the organizer of this venture and would have it timed to the minute and budgeted to the penny.

Cora hugged each of her friends with a one-armed embrace, unwilling to relinquish her bow, lest it fall prey to some "accident." She allowed Benedict to kiss her hand, then addressed all three of them.

"I'm astonished to see you all. I thought you'd determined it was too great an expense in both time and money."

"Yes, well, you know Harriet," Jane replied. "She found a discount on train tickets if we traveled at exactly the right time. Benedict has an old college friend he can stay with, and we'll simply stay with you for a couple of days."

Cora's fingers clenched around her bow. No one entering her room now would have any inkling that only days ago she'd been living with a man in scandalous fashion. And she'd shared quarters with her friends on any number of occasions. Even so, the idea of letting anyone but Adam into that space filled her with a sick sense of wrongness. He should have been here.

Wear this flower, and I'll be with you, even if you can't see me.

She'd spent half a night sobbing over his brief note, clutching the gift he'd left her. That ought to have been enough. A few days at a distance should have allowed any infatuation to wane. She'd expected by now to be settling back into their original friendship, where an exchange of letters would satisfy her. It wouldn't.

"And as for the time commitment," Benedict added, "I decided the journey was of sufficient importance to merit a few days away from work."

Cora clutched a hand over her unsettled stomach. "I can't marry you," she blurted.

"What?" He gaped at her.

"I'm sorry. Excuse me, I need to collect my arrows, and then I have to go… somewhere else."

"Cora." Benedict reached a hand toward her. "I didn't… I wasn't…"

"What's wrong?" Jane asked.

"Has something happened?" Harriet asked at the same time.

Cora could only shake her head and hurry off toward the target. She couldn't discuss this. Not now. Not with her heart aching over Adam and her competition in two days.

Her friends jogged after her.

"Cora, that wasn't what I meant about being important," Benedict called. His long stride quickly caught up to her. "I wouldn't want to pressure you before your tournament."

Before. But what about after? She didn't want him to propose then. Or ever. Right now, though, she couldn't find the words to explain. His presence was too sudden, too surprising. She needed space.

"Please excuse me," she said again. "I wasn't prepared for visitors. I need a bit of time to get ready."

Three worried pairs of eyes stared at her.

"If you give me a few hours, I can meet you for dinner," Cora promised. That would be enough time to compose herself and gather her thoughts. She hoped. "Meet me at the east end of the Pike."

"Six-thirty, sharp," Harriet insisted.

"I'll see you then." Stuffing her arrows into her quiver, Cora hurried off.

The moment she was out of earshot, her heart rate began to slow. She was overreacting. This wasn't so bad. It would be nice to have friends to cheer her on. It only hurt because Adam wouldn't be among them.

Thompson and his pal had wandered off to join a cluster of other men just outside the field, by the gymnasium. Cora headed around the building to avoid them, but paused just past the corner when she heard one of the men say, "…energetic bout of bedsport the night before a competition."

"Ridiculous," another man scoffed.

"Not at all," the first man argued. "I do it every time. Wake up in the morning feeling relaxed and undistracted by any sexual urges."

Cora peeked around the corner.

"Terrible idea," grumbled a red-headed man with a deep voice. "I've abstained for a full month leading up to this event. Can't go about wasting energy in sexual excess. Makes a body weak. Save that sort of thing until after."

"Your poor wife," snorted the first man who had spoken. "Bet she's taking advantage of your absence right about now." He reached into his pocket and pulled out a large handful of small paper packages. One fluttered to the ground, but he didn't notice. "For the rest of you, I've got sheaths you can use. Trust me on this. Find yourself a girl and have a tumble." He started handing out the packets to the men. "Shoot at night to shoot better the next day, eh?"

Cora darted out from behind the building and snatched up the condom the man had dropped. The paper wrapping had been printed with the words "St. Louis 1904" and an image of an arrow stuck into a target. Cora stuffed it into her pocket. She'd save it for the next time she saw Adam. If she ever saw him again.

I will. Someday, I will.

She slipped a hand in her pocket and fingered the small package. Why should the male athletes be the only ones allowed to have any fun? *She* wanted to test whether sexual activity the night before a competition improved performance. If only Adam were here.

Someday, she vowed. She wouldn't let a perfectly good contraceptive go to waste.

. . . ⟶ . . .

"This is delightfully creepy," Harriet remarked. The small group made their way through a mirror-filled gallery that ushered visitors into the Hereafter attraction. Somewhere in the distance echoed the shrieks and groans of the damned—or whatever poor souls had been recruited to play the denizens of Hades.

"It's... interesting," Cora replied. Even with Adam safely away, the old worries about something malfunctioning made it difficult to properly enjoy the attraction. The evening with her friends had been pleasant so far. Dinner had been excellent, with talk of the food and the fair, and no mentions of Cora's outburst from earlier.

She'd caught a few anxious glances in her direction, though, and Benedict had been talking more around her than to her. She needed to find an opportunity to explain why she had no intention of ever marrying him.

And then there was Doyle, who'd run across her three times today and had now attached himself to their group. Was he following her? If it turned out he was the one who had caused all the trouble, she was going to be sick. And then she would pummel him for Adam's sake.

She fidgeted through the entire first portion of the attraction, a disappearing-persons illusion that ought to have intrigued her. Her unsettled mind refused to focus.

"Harriet and I will sit together," Jane insisted, as the group loaded into the small boats that would carry them through the remainder of the Hereafter. "You and Benedict can sit behind us." She winked at Cora, then leaned in to whisper, "You can talk things over. I'm sure it's not too late to work everything out."

Jane would only be thwarted in her desire to see her cousin and her friend together, but Cora nodded. Sitting with Benedict would provide the opening she needed.

Ignoring the skeletons dropping from the ceiling and continued screams of the lost souls in hell, Cora took her seat in the boat beside Benedict.

"We need to talk," she whispered. "I know you would like to press your courtship, but I must tell you that I cannot possibly marry you."

"I understand you're an unconventional woman," he replied. "But is the thought of marriage so repugnant to you?"

"No. I'm not against marriage with the right man. But we don't suit. To be perfectly frank, I have absolutely no interest in engaging in sexual activity with you."

"Cora!" he gasped, though she hadn't spoken loud enough for anyone else to hear. He shuffled a little closer to her. "It's not something you need be afraid of," he whispered. "When I kiss you more, you will begin to understand."

"No!"

"Are you quite all right, Miss Maxwell?" Doyle asked from behind her. "Not upset by the terrors of hell, are you?"

Cora glanced at a tableau of a robber being rebuffed time and again as he attempted to spend his ill-gotten gains.

"Not at all, thank you," she called. She lowered her voice again and spoke to Benedict. "I don't want to kiss you. Ever. But it's more than that. We lack an intimate connection. I don't want to go running to tell you first when I learn something new. I have no desire to snuggle close to you and whisper all my hopes and dreams. I can't imagine sitting across from you at breakfast every morning and dinner every night. I don't long to share my victories with you."

Cora could picture only one man in the scenarios she'd just described. One man she longed to see night and day. One man who made her body sing and her heart soar. Who made her smile and laugh and who brought her a sense of peace and happiness.

She jerked so forcefully her hand splashed into the water beside the boat. Her heart began to thud. The truth surged through her with a sudden, irrefutable certainty. She was in love with Adam Levett. Not infatuated, not merely lustful. Genuinely, deeply in love. There'd been no zing, no magic fairytale moment, just a growing sense of rightness. One she hadn't fully grasped until now.

Now, when he was far away and she had no hope of telling him all that was in her heart. Tears sprang unbidden to her eyes.

"There's someone else, isn't there?" Benedict asked. "You've fallen in love." He jerked a thumb at Doyle. "It's not him, is it?"

"No." Cora chuckled. "But, yes, there is, and yes, I have."

"Huh. Not interested in love, myself. I was hoping for quiet, uncomplicated regard. I thought you were the same, but apparently not."

"No, I'm not. I want passion. I always have. Sorry."

He shrugged one shoulder. "My mistake. Best to find out now, I suppose. I hope we can still be friends."

A warm glow of happiness radiated throughout her entire body. So much in the world remained wrong, but this was right. "I would like that."

She turned her focus back to the ride just in time to see a man with horns and a pointed tail leap out at the passing boat. Steam billowed from hidden vents as the fictional Satan snarled, threatening the passersby. Cora suppressed a giggle. How utterly ridiculous.

Jane and Harriet, as members of the large section of humanity who seemed to enjoy frightening themselves, yelped in delighted horror and pretended to cover their eyes. Behind Cora, Doyle let out a startled, and amusingly appropriate, "Damnation!" Moments later, the boat tumbled down a small water slide and into Paradise.

Heaven was… underwhelming. Pretty to look upon, but one could only stand so many sparkling stars and singing angels. When the boat reached its final destination, Cora was the first to hop out.

"Well, I think I'm ready to head home. Competition starts in two days. Have to get some rest."

Mostly, she just wanted to be back in her room, with pen and paper in hand, writing a lengthy and gushing love letter to Adam. Or in bed with her eyes closed, dreaming of him.

Fortunately, the rest of the group, weary from travel, agreed it was time to turn in. Benedict excused himself, giving Cora a polite bow rather than another kiss on the hand. Doyle vanished without a word, and Jane and Harriet each happily took hold of one of Cora's arms.

Right. They were staying with her. In all her worry over her romantic life, she'd all but forgotten.

"You and Benedict seemed cozy on the ride," Jane cooed.

"Yes. We had a lovely discussion about how we are best suited as friends."

Jane's brows furrowed. "Friends?"

"Indeed. And that's exactly how I want it. I'm very pleased."

"Well, and that's what matters most," Harriet replied. "Now, about the fair. Aren't all the lights just stunning?"

To Cora's great relief, no one said another word about love or men the remainder of the way to the hotel. By the time she waved her friends into her room, she was as happy and relaxed as she'd been in days. She still missed Adam fiercely, but life was good and she was constructing a new vision for the future.

"Ooh, Cora," Harriet gasped. "This metal flower is exquisite. Wherever did you get it?" She reached for the battery-powered flower Cora had left behind on her desk when she'd put away her archery equipment earlier in the day. Harriet's hand paused in midair, hovering over the condom Cora had also left lying in plain sight. "And what is this peculiar little package?"

"Um…" Cora rushed to scoop up her possessions. Her friends eyed her curiously. "You know Mr. Levett, who I have exchanged all those letters with?"

Jane and Harriet shared a puzzled look, then turned back to Cora. "Yes?"

"Well…" Clutching her treasures, Cora took a deep breath. And told them everything.

21

Excerpt of a letter from Mr. Adam Levett to Miss Cora Maxwell, dated May 17th, 1904

I'm so thrilled to hear that you'll be competing in St. Louis! I will be there much of the summer working the AutomaTech booth. I'll arrange my stay to last through September. Nothing will keep me from being there to watch!

Sept. 18

"Y OU LOOK RIDICULOUS, you know."

Adam didn't lower the binoculars. From the far end of the athletic field, he could see Cora's back as she aimed her bow at the target. Her friends sat in the stands, observing her practice and clapping when she made a good shot. Which, naturally, was most of the time.

"She's going to see you and then she's going to be furious," Doyle continued.

"I only want to make sure she's safe and that nothing is going to get between her and that gold medal."

"Bullshit. You just can't stay away. Guess I've skipped work and put my own career at risk for no good reason."

Adam did lower the binoculars now and looked at his friend, shaking his head. "Don't think I didn't see you picking up pamphlets from every single engineering company at the fair."

Doyle smirked. "I've organized them by who pays the most."

"You'll end up one of those cleaning rat sellers." Adam returned to his surveillance. Doyle was absolutely correct. He couldn't stay away. Surrounded by her friends and the other women's archery competitors, Cora was in little danger. Her reputation appeared unharmed. She didn't need him here. But he couldn't bring himself to leave.

A few more minutes. That's all he needed. Then he'd go hide out for the rest of the day and return in the morning to watch her competition. He wasn't missing that, no matter how many newspapers bad-mouthed him. He'd hide quietly in a far corner of the stands, if necessary, but he was going to see her win come hell or high water.

"Well, if it isn't the bookish boyfriend."

Adam spun around, letting the binoculars fall to hang from the strap around his neck. He fumbled in his pocket for his spectacles.

"Thompson, wasn't it?" Adam asked. The obnoxious man was strolling by along with half-a-dozen other men, all with bows in their hands and quivers slung over their shoulders. Competitors in men's archery, come to displace the ladies in favor of their own practice.

Thompson made a curt nod. "Or is it ex-boyfriend? Has she thrown you over for that well-dressed fellow?"

Adam automatically looked down at his clothing. The top button of his vest was undone, and his shirt was wrinkled. His head snapped back up. Dammit. He shouldn't let this bastard get to him.

"Whomever Miss Maxwell wishes to befriend is her own business," he replied primly. "Not yours. And I'd thank you not to harass her simply because you were unable to defeat her without cheating."

"What's that?" chimed in one of the other men. "Didn't you say she challenged you and you politely turned her down?"

"They squared off right over there." Adam pointed in the direction of Cora's old practice area. "I witnessed the entire thing. Mr. Thompson was losing and resorted to cheating. Nothing polite or gentlemanly about it. I believe Miss Maxwell is still waiting for her apology."

Thompson's face had turned a mottled crimson. "You think you're so smart, don't you? Well, let me tell you something you don't know. That girl you're so enamored of? She's nothing special. Just some chit who thinks she's an athlete because once she hit a few bullseyes. The minute things get tough, she'll crumble."

Hah! Cora, crumble? Never.

"I promise you, Thompson," Adam said coolly, "Miss Maxwell has more tenacity in her little finger than your mind can even comprehend. She has the heart of a champion, and you can't touch that, no matter how you belittle her. But I'm sure insulting her to your friends makes you feel big and manly, so don't let me stop you."

Thompson jabbed a finger into Adam's chest. "Just you wait. This competition won't be some children's game. And when she falls apart, you'll be the only sorry fan left cheering." He spun away and stormed off.

"That was maybe not the best way to handle that encounter," Adam sighed, when the archers had all passed out of hearing range.

"No," Doyle agreed. "I'm sure he deserved it. But you and trouble. Thick as thieves."

Adam hauled himself up onto the railing. "I'm going over there in case he tries something."

Doyle grabbed Adam by the coat. "Oh, no, you're not. You're going back across the river to your little hideout and you're going to wait for this to blow over. No more chaos. I like that girl, Levett. She's good for you, and I'm not going to let you muck this up. Go buy her some flowers and a diamond ring. After she wins, *then* you can come popping out of the stands to surprise her. At that point she'll be too happy to be furious at you. Then you go down on one knee and swear your undying love."

Adam tried and failed not to envision the scenario. In one version, she flung her arms around him and kissed him in front of the entire crowd. In the other, she slapped him across the face. "Cora is eminently capable of being both happy and furious at the same time."

"See? You know her so well. You're perfect for one another. Now shoo. 'No trouble before her competition.' That is exactly what you told me. You go home, I'll go watch out for her."

Reluctantly, Adam slid down from the rail. "Phone my hotel if anything happens."

· · · ✤ · · ·

The phone never rang, despite the long hours Adam spent sitting in the hotel lobby, staring at it, prepared to race to Cora's rescue at a moment's notice. He checked at the front desk half a dozen times throughout the day, but no messages came for him. When he finally departed the next morning, he suspected the staff was more than happy to see the back of him.

He fidgeted the entire train ride into St. Louis. It was happening. Cora was competing in the Olympic Games today. The entire world would know of her. How in hell was he going to manage to make it through the day without expiring from nerves? She would be calm as ever, he expected. Maybe he was the storage vessel for all her anxiety.

Here, let me hold that for you while you compete.

He sighed. If he'd already been with her, he could have said these things aloud and made her laugh. It had been a full week since he'd heard her laugh. Too long.

The stands at the athletic field were crowded with people who'd come to watch the in-progress men's competition. Adam hurried up the steps to the top of the bleachers and dropped into an empty seat.

The event was sadly boring when he had zero interest in the outcome. The men fired arrow after arrow, and it seemed to drag on forever. Instead of watching the archers, he watched the outskirts of the stadium, looking for Cora.

She appeared near the end of the event, along with several other women archers. They leaned against the rail, cooly observing their male counterparts. Cora looked divine. Most of the other women wore full length sleeves, but she'd once again chosen the sleeveless white dress. A simple brown corset covered her torso. It would be tied tight enough to support, but not enough to impede her breathing or her movement. The memory of unlacing that very corset and peeling it from her body shivered through him. God, what he wouldn't give to hold her in his arms again.

Cora reached up to fix a pin in her hairdo. A bit of metal glinted in the sunlight. Adam's breath caught in his throat. The flower. She was wearing it. He hopped up from his seat and shuffled down the row, apologizing to people as he squeezed by. He had to get closer. He had to be certain.

He'd just found himself a new seat with a reasonable view of her when the crowd began to applaud. The men's event was over. A judge announced the final scores through an electronic loudspeaker that sounded unpleasantly like the blaring one at the AutomaTech booth. Medals were presented to the three top competitors. Thompson came in fourth, Adam noted with a grin.

No medal for you, you cheating, woman-hating scum.

Some of the crowd departed with the men, but a large percentage remained to watch the women compete. Adam moved several rows closer. Yes, Cora was definitely wearing his flower. His skin prickled. Maybe Doyle's advice hadn't been complete nonsense. Maybe buying flowers and a diamond ring would have been a good idea.

Propose to Cora. Make her mine forever.

Dear God, did he crave that. To wake up with her every morning. Kiss her every day. Make love to her... well, realistically probably not every night, but certainly very often.

Down on the field, Olympic officials moved targets, checked equipment, and prepared for the event to begin. Cora, as she had been during practices, was positioned closest to the grandstand. She wiped sweat from her brow and took a long drink from a small jug of water. The temperature was warm, but not scorching. Perhaps she was more nervous than he'd expected.

"Give all your fear to me," he murmured. "Let me take it from you. You just do what you do."

The man sitting beside him gave him a confused look.

The loudspeaker crackled on again. "Welcome to the Ladies' Double Columbia Round. The competitors will be shooting forty-eight arrows at each of fifty, forty, and thirty yards. Please welcome the competitors. From the Cincinnati Archery Club, Miss Taylor, Mrs. Woodruff—"

Adam never heard the remainder of the names, because down on the field, Cora suddenly staggered. She put a hand to her head, took one more stumbling step, then fell.

"Cora!"

He sprang from his seat and dashed down the bleachers, hopping rows and dodging other spectators. Cora regained her feet, but swayed woozily. What was wrong? What had happened to her? Caring nothing for propriety or protocol, he vaulted over the wall to the grass and ran to her side.

"Cora! Are you all right?"

"Adam?" She blinked at him, then a dreamy smile crossed her lips. The same sort of sleepy, half-dazed smile she'd given him after he'd pleasured her to multiple climaxes. "Adam! You're here!" Her smile faded to a puzzled frown. "Why do you look so shimmery? And why is the ground moving? Is it swaying to the music? Do you hear that?"

"Hear what?"

Her only response was to topple into his arms.

22

Excerpt of a letter from Miss Cora Maxwell to Mr. Adam Levett, dated June 6, 1904

I had the most peculiar dream last night, and I simply have to share it with you. I had just finished a competition, but instead of handing me a trophy or medal, all the judges went down on one knee in front of me with engagement rings. I was terribly embarrassed to have to turn them all down, but then you walked over and presented me with an Electro-Flex...

ADAM WAS HERE! Delight raced through Cora, tempered by a touch of confusion. Why was he here? And what were they doing? It seemed unlike him to be holding her so close in front of this crowd of people.

And he was certainly close. Warmth radiated from his body. He must have just shaved, because her nose caught a whiff of lemon scent from the soap he used. His arms held her tight, fortunately, because the world seemed in constant motion around her.

Everything was a whirl of sound and color, like the music

and dancing along the Pike, but magnified. A lilting tune echoed through the air, and colored shapes fluttered past in every direction. Were those colors some trick of the light, or were they people in wild, bright clothing, spinning in an endless dance?

"What's happened?" a distant voice asked. "Has she taken ill?"

"I fear she may have been poisoned." Adam's voice, oddly distorted. "What was in that jug?"

What on earth was he talking about? Who? Cora didn't see any poison or any jug. Only people. So many people, bounding past, singing, chattering. Why was Adam embracing her in front of all these people? He didn't do that. He was worried about her reputation.

She certainly didn't want to leave his arms, though. He felt so perfect against her. Like everything she'd ever wanted.

"I love you," she sighed.

Love, yes. That made sense. Maybe this was their wedding party! That would explain everything. The colors, the music, the improper public hugging. She'd clearly had too much to drink in her excitement. How odd, that they'd chosen such an elaborate celebration. She couldn't recall why they'd done that. Strangely, she couldn't recall any vows, either, or even a proposal. All the sounds and lights were confusing her.

"Take me home," she begged. "I want to be alone with you."

Adam didn't respond. Didn't move. Had he even heard her? It was so loud here, and her head was pounding.

"Adam? Please take me home."

"Cora," he said at last. His voice still had a peculiar congested quality to it, as if it were coming to her through water instead of air. "Cora, can you hear me?"

"Y-yes." Now her own voice sounded odd.

"Cora." A hand stroked her cheek, scorching hot against her skin. She gasped.

"Cora, I need you to look at me. Please try."

"I don't understand." She *was* looking at him. True, he faded in and out somewhat, with all those distracting colored swirls blurring her vision.

The hand brushed her cheek again, gentle fire that seemed to come from a place outside reality.

"Open your eyes, love," Adam crooned. "Look at me, Cora. You can do it."

She blinked. Sunlight blinded her, and she buried her head against Adam's chest. Real. Solid. The only thing she could cling to in this strange jumble of the world.

"That's it." His fingers grazed the underside of her chin, slowly tilting her face up to his. "Stay with me. I have some clean water here. I want you to sip it slowly. Can you do that?"

He touched the jug to her lips, and a trickle of cool water ran into her mouth and down her throat. She gulped, and swallowed.

"Here, try some brandy," another male voice suggested. Benedict?

"No, give her my coffee." That was Jane. Where had everyone come from?

Warm steam wafted before her face, carrying with it the bracing aroma of strong coffee. Cora took one sip, then another. She'd downed half the cup before she realized what she was doing. Her eyelids fluttered, her eyes opening properly wide for the first time in what seemed like hours.

"Drink the rest of it," Jane insisted. "It's helping."

Cora lifted her hand to grasp the cup herself, but before she could get a grip her stomach gave a horrifying lurch.

"I feel… I feel…" She shoved herself out of Adam's arms, stumbled a few steps, and retched.

Sinking to the ground, she emptied the entire contents of her breakfast into the grass, and perhaps some of last night's dinner too. By the time her stomach settled, her throat burned and her muscles ached. Tears of discomfort streamed down her cheeks. She wiped them away with the back of her hand, gasping for breath.

Her vision had cleared. No more loud music or dancing colors. The world had fallen still and quiet. The only people were her friends clustered around her and the spectators in the stands, watching in stunned silence.

"Oh, my God!" she burst out. "The Games! My event!" She scrambled to her feet, wobbling until Adam grabbed her arm to steady her.

"Cora. It'll be okay. You've probably rid yourself of most of the poison. Let's find somewhere you can sit and rest. We'll get you more water and the rest of the coffee. But drink slowly this time."

Again, she pulled away from him, taking slow, deliberate steps. Her legs trembled, hardly able to support her. Her arms hung heavy at her sides. Even lifting her bow would be difficult.

"I'm here to compete," she proclaimed. Carefully, she bent to retrieve her fallen bow. "No one is going to take that from me."

Adam nodded. Took a step back. Behind his spectacles, his hazel eyes shimmered. "Whatever you want. I'll be here if you need me."

"Miss Maxwell?" a judge in an austere black suit asked. "Are you well enough to participate?"

"Yes," she said defiantly, though she felt anything but.

"Very good. Please signal for one of us if at any time you are unable to continue."

Cora drank more water and the remainder of the coffee while the officials made announcements and declared the event ready to begin. Adam and her friends retreated to the stands, taking front row seats others had graciously vacated. Adam leaned forward against the wall, looking ready to leap down to her side at any moment.

What was he doing here? She'd told him to stay away! Annoyance warred with delight. She touched the flower in her hair. He was here, despite any potential danger to himself. Here to support her, whether by catching her when she fell ill or cheering from the stands.

It didn't matter that her stomach felt turned inside-out, or that every limb ached. No matter the throbbing headache. She was shooting for him, and she would give it her all. When the signal came, she lifted her bow and took aim.

. . . ⤳ . . .

Her final arrow caught the outer edge of the red circle. Cora let out a long breath of relief. She hadn't shot well, by her usual standards, but she'd persevered and finished, despite the aches in her limbs and the pounding in her head. Her stomach had significantly improved, and hunger, not sickness, now gnawed at her. In the stands, her friends waved and cheered. She lifted a hand in acknowledgement.

The crackling loudspeaker clicked back on, and a judge announced the final scores. "In third place, with a total of six hundred thirty points, Miss Cora Maxwell."

A small flying dragon swooped over to her, a bronze medal dangling from its beak. Cora accepted the medal, pinning it to her dress. It wasn't the gold she'd wanted, but she was damned proud of it, regardless.

The dragon flew off to deliver the silver and gold medals. Cora waited to shake hands with all of the other women, congratulating them on their performances, and blushing when they complimented both her shooting and her tenacity.

With the event concluded at last, she made her way to her waiting fans, weary but content. Food and a rest would restore her to her usual self. Tomorrow she would shoot again, and she would be unstoppable.

"I'm sorry you didn't get the gold, Cora," Harriet said, catching Cora's hand and giving it a small squeeze. "But I'm so impressed with how well you competed while ill."

"Yes. Dashed fine shooting," Benedict added. He glanced at Adam. "Though Mr. Levett says he's seen you do better."

Cora could read the unspoken question in Benedict's expression. *Him?*

She nodded. "I was tired and unsteady. Tomorrow you'll see what I'm really capable of."

Adam came to stand beside her, gently touching her elbow. "Cora, where did your jug of water come from? I'm worried it might have been tainted."

Cora considered the possibility. She couldn't remember whether she'd noticed a funny taste. The time before she'd taken ill was a bit of a blur.

"I think it was on a table over there, where we entered," she replied, pointing. "Water was provided for every contestant."

"Provided by whom?" Jane asked. "I don't recall the men having any water." She rubbed a finger across her lips. "Seems suspicious. And I don't remember you eating anything unusual at breakfast."

"Why don't we ask the men about it?" Benedict started off without waiting for anyone else. "There's a group of them still milling about down there."

Cora hurried after him, Adam keeping close to her side. His presence comforted her. Her legs weren't nearly as wobbly as before, but they'd yet to regain their full steadiness.

"I don't understand how you can continue to argue against this," Condom Man was saying, tapping the gold medal pinned to his chest. His other hand held a fistful of his custom-branded contraceptives. "It's a fact. I performed best. If you gentlemen had spent last evening in the company of a willing woman, you would've—" He broke off when he spied Cora and her friends approaching.

"Afternoon, fellas," Benedict said cheerily. "Quick question for you. Were you all provided water for the competition? Seems the ladies were and I wondered if that's customary for all athletes or a special accommodation due to their sex?"

Most of the men regarded him curiously. Cora kept her eyes on Thompson. He was her primary suspect.

"*I* didn't get any water," the red-headed anti-sex man replied. "Any of you?"

Several mumbled, "No."

"You, Thompson?" Adam challenged, striding toward him. "Do you happen to know anything about water jugs suspiciously appearing for the women?"

Cora wished she knew more about reading body language. How could she tell if he was lying? Twitches? Looking away?

Thompson merely scowled, like always. "Why would I?"

"Oh, I don't know." Adam's voice was even, but he radiated fury. Cora could read *him*, certainly. He stood rigid as a stone, fingers curled into fists, eyes blazing. "Maybe because you hold a grudge against Miss Maxwell? Maybe because you cheated before and I can't imagine your behavior has improved any since?"

"Maybe *you* should keep your damned prissy nose out of other people's business."

"What did you do to her?" Adam snarled.

"Maybe she's just not as good as you think she is," Thompson scoffed.

Adam folded his arms across his chest. "Oh? Where's *your* medal?"

Several men snickered. Harriet coughed to cover a laugh.

"I'd like to see you try to shoot while poisoned," Adam continued. "And even if she'd come in last, it wouldn't matter. She is so far above you, you're not even worthy to lick the scum from the soles of her boots."

"And you are?" Thompson laughed. "Don't cry when she takes up with Mr. Fancy Suit." He gestured at Benedict. "Or with that blond man who was hanging around all day yesterday."

Adam squared his shoulders. "If you think I'd have any less

admiration for her because she makes her own life decisions, you're even stupider than I thought."

Cora blinked against the sudden wateriness of her eyes. Ripping into Thompson herself might have been satisfying, but nothing could compare to Adam's righteous anger. She loved his willingness to fight for her. His unwavering support. His respect and affection for everything she was. How had it taken her so long to realize no other man could compete with him in her heart?

Thompson's left hand flew at Adam, who dodged easily, not realizing it was merely a feint. Thompson was right-handed, a detail Adam would never have noticed. Cora cried out, but she was too late. Thompson's right fist crashed into Adam's face, sending him reeling. Blood trickled from his nose. Several pairs of hands grabbed the two men, dragging them apart.

Cora's entire body burned with rage. She darted between the men and slammed her fist into Thompson's groin as hard as she could.

The *flash-pop* of a camera going off made her whirl around. The reporter from the night of the blackout stood grinning at the turmoil, camera in hand and notebook jutting from a vest pocket.

"Thanks, Lord of Chaos," he said. He chuckled, tipped his hat, and raced off.

Cora didn't pause, didn't think, just broke into a flat-out run. "Stop that man!"

23

Excerpt of a letter from Mr. Adam Levett to Miss Cora Maxwell, dated September 10, 1903

I regret to inform you that I'm a terribly boring sort of man. I spend most of my time either drawing, playing with tools, or doing mathematical calculations. I will have to live vicariously through your tales of travel and competitions.

ADAM SPRINTED AFTER the slanderous reporter like an Olympic track athlete, flying past the athletic field until they stumbled out onto the wide expanse of the road dubbed Olympian Way. A mass of motorcars hummed and puffed steam, chugging ponderously down the road in neatly-arranged rows.

The auto race! Good God.

Adam staggered to a halt and threw out an arm to catch Cora before she could run into danger. Some twenty cars ambled along, looking like nothing more than ordinary road cars out on a Sunday drive. Adam knew better. These cars had been fine-tuned and modified, and at any moment they'd fly off as wildly as any specialized racing vehicle.

A pistol shot rent the air and engines roared as the cars began to accelerate. The reporter, still clutching his camera, leapt onto the small luggage rack at the back of a huffing steam car, hunkering down to hide himself from the driver.

"You won't get away with this, you bastard!" Cora shouted.

A gleaming motorcar with no discernible steam engine drew alongside Cora and Adam. A dark-haired man with most of his face obscured by driving goggles smirked at them. "If you want to catch him, hop aboard."

Cora didn't hesitate, and Adam didn't see how he had any choice but to follow her. He'd barely stepped into the rear seat when the car lurched forward, sending him toppling into her lap.

For a moment, he lay stunned, one hand splayed across her thigh, his face inches from the swells of her breasts.

"Oh, Adam," she murmured, running her fingers through his hair.

He stared at her, unable to think of any good reason he shouldn't ravish her right this instant in the back of a moving motorcar.

"Is your nose all right?" she asked.

The question shook him out of his lustful stupor, and he clambered properly into his seat, lifting a hand gingerly to his face. A small trickle of blood still dripped, and he wiped it away with his sleeve.

"It hurts, but I don't think it's broken." He took a moment to glance at the scenery whizzing past him. This automobile was remarkably fast and had already overtaken a number of its competitors. "I'd meant to watch this race, not participate in it."

The driver chuckled. "I see your quarry up ahead. Who is the villain in this play, you or him?"

"Him, obviously," Cora answered indignantly.

"Pity."

The car carrying the reporter and a few others that

remained ahead of them disappeared around a corner. Their own ride barreled toward the turn at top speed.

Adam clutched the door. "Shouldn't we slow down?"

"I have calculated the precise speed at which this vehicle can make each turn of this course," the driver replied haughtily. "You, of course, have changed the equations by adding to the overall weight, but I've made adjustments in my head since you climbed aboard."

Adam reached for Cora's hand and their fingers entwined tightly. They were going to die. They were in the car of a madman.

The car flew around the corner, slowing—somewhat—at what must have been the last possible second before making the turn and roaring back to top speed.

Cora's grip on Adam's hand loosened. "That was excellently done. Look how much distance we've gained on a single turn."

And they had. Adam did some quick mental calculations of his own. A few more turns and they would be in the lead. Given what he remembered about the course and the number of laps, this car would easily win. The other vehicles would have to become much more aggressive on the turns to have a chance.

Cora shifted in her seat, bringing her thigh in contact with his. She leaned toward him, and when he turned toward her, the adoring gleam in her eyes took his breath away. His heart, which had only begun to slow from the harrowing turn, began to race again.

"I hope we catch him," she whispered. "I want to catch him so much. For you. But even if we don't, I love having an adventure with you."

"I was never an adventure-having sort of man until you came along," Adam replied. Lord, did he want to pull her into his arms and kiss her senseless. Newspapers be damned. He'd take chaos if he got Cora in exchange. "But now I wouldn't have it any other way."

He was a mere inch from giving into temptation and

capturing her lips when the motorcar slewed around another corner and he had to clutch the door so as not to topple from his seat.

"Why the hell do they not make straps to hold you down in these cursed things?" he wondered.

"Ruins the fun for the spectators," the driver replied. "The more possibility for violent death, the better. I fail to understand it, myself. If I wanted to see death, I could walk the streets of New York."

"Who *are* you?" Adam wondered.

The man only chuckled.

Up ahead, the reporter still sat perched on the back of the steam car, not looking back, as far as Adam could tell. Did he not realize how close they were? By the end of this lap, they'd be neck-and-neck.

And then what? Did he shout at the other man? Leap foolishly from one moving vehicle to another?

No. He liked adventures with Cora, but preferred ones that would allow him to continue to have future adventures.

Eventually, Adam's estimates proved correct. The final turn back onto Olympian Way closed the remaining gap between this automobile and the steam cars ahead of it. Their driver brought them up alongside the car with the reporter, waving his hand in an ostentatious flourish.

"Your villain."

"You there!" Adam shouted, at the same time Cora called out, "Give up, you lying scoundrel!"

The reporter stared at them for a moment, then his eyes darted back and forth, seeking an escape. He had none. The cars could continue on exactly side-by-side until the end of the race. He was a stowaway, so his driver certainly wouldn't be stopping to help him.

"Toss me the camera now and maybe Miss Maxwell won't punch your lights out at the end of the race," Adam yelled.

The reporter responded by taking another photograph.

Scum. But he had no way out. A little patience and Adam could catch him and interrogate him. The steam car began to slow, approaching the first turn. Damn. Adam would have to beg their driver not to get too far ahead. They needed to keep their enemy in sight.

"Adam!" Cora grabbed his arm, gasping in horror as the reporter used the reduced speed to leap from the back of the moving vehicle. He tumbled into an awkward somersault, narrowly missing the wheels of another car.

"My God," Adam gasped. Without thinking he clapped his hand down on their driver's shoulder. "Stop. Let us out."

"And lose all the ground I've gained?" He shrugged Adam off. "What do you think this is, a taxicab?"

Adam opened his mouth to plead further, when the car slowed abruptly, pitching him forward nearly into the front seat.

"Excellent brakes, don't you think?" the driver chuckled.

Adam didn't reply, simply seized Cora's hand and jumped down to the ground, sprinting in the direction the reporter had taken. He'd been limping after his wild leap. They could catch him.

"See you in the papers tomorrow!" The voice was nearly drowned out beneath the sound of the departing motorcar.

"Where did he go?" Cora fretted, craning her neck to look as they pushed past the crowd of people lining the streets to watch the motorcar race.

"I can see him," Adam assured her, not taking his eyes off the staggering man. "He's still stunned from the fall. We'll catch—" He yelped as a small child darted into his path and he stumbled to one side to avoid a collision. Cora banged into him.

"Watch where you're going," a woman scolded. "Honestly. Running down a public thoroughfare? How appalling."

Adam had to force himself not to stop and apologize. Gad. This certainly wasn't going to ease any of the Lord of Chaos talk.

Cora yanked on his hand. "There! There he is. Come on!"

Together they hurried down the street, walking and sometimes jogging as fast as they were able through the crowds. They made up some ground, but the man they were chasing appeared to be recovering and had picked up his own pace as well. How long could they keep this up?

Beside him, Cora was breathing hard. Adam mumbled a curse. She shouldn't be doing this. Not after the morning she'd had. She needed to be resting. Recovering. Preparing for tomorrow's competition. His long strides began to falter.

"No, don't stop, we almost have him," she begged, lengthening her own stride and pulling on his arm. "I won't let him get away with doing this to you."

"Cora. Don't hurt yourself."

"I *will* stop him," she vowed, and raced on, determined. Unstoppable.

Adam loped beside her. That was it, then. He wouldn't leave her, and he'd catch her if she fell, but he wouldn't force her. She'd chosen her own path. And somehow, miraculously, she'd chosen *him*. She was pushing herself, putting aside her own goals to save him. It was the most humbling experience of his entire life.

I'm not worth it, he almost said, before thinking better of it. Dammit, if she wanted him, as a friend, lover, or anything else, he would *be* worth it. He would be the best, loudest, most passionate fan she would ever have.

Their enemy was running out of both time and space. The Grand Basin lay just ahead, and in this crowded area of the fair he'd be unable to outmaneuver them much longer. He veered suddenly toward the water, pushing through a crowd waiting to board the decorative boats that trolled the pond.

Shoving aside a woman in an enormous flowered hat, he vaulted over a rail and into one of the swan-shaped crafts and shoved at the throttle. The boat roared to life. All across the dock, people shouted and pointed, but Cora and Adam squeezed through the startled throng, rushing past the ticket counter and jumping into a long narrow boat fashioned in the style of a serpentine dragon.

Adam stabbed a finger in the direction of the fleeing reporter. "Follow that swan!"

24

Excerpt of a letter from Mr. Adam Levett to Miss Cora Maxwell, dated September 10, 1903

Who knows, perhaps someday we'll meet and have an adventure together.

"**N**OW SEE HERE!" the boat's captain demanded, to no real effect, as Cora had already begun tugging the rope from its moorings.

"We'll pay afterward," Adam promised, wincing at the sudden pang of guilt. He was causing a ruckus. Making a scene. Engaging in possibly criminal activity. Proving himself the Lord of Chaos in his attempt to disprove it. Ouch.

"How do I make this go?" Cora reached for the control panel, but the captain jumped to stop her.

"Throttle, rudder, speed, heading." Adam began pointing out various dials and instruments, and Cora stretched a hand past the boatman.

"I'm going! I'm going!" he protested, setting the boat into motion. "Darned fool kids."

The engine at the rear of the vehicle chugged. Steam puffed

out through the dragon's nostrils, carried by long copper pipes running along the sides of the boat and up to its metal head. They drifted away from the dock. Peacefully. Leisurely.

Cora glared at the controls. "Can't this thing go any faster?"

Adam's gaze darted to the reporter in the swan boat. He wasn't faring any better, and from the looks of it, he wasn't especially adept with the controls.

"This is a pleasure craft, miss," the captain grumbled. "If you'd wanted a race, you ought to have gone to see the motorcars."

Adam and Cora turned to face one another, laughing together. The captain muttered something else about "kids these days."

The dragon snorted again, its twitching tail steering it toward its prey. Ahead of them, the swan released a hiss of steam from its mouth. Both craft sailed sleepily on.

"These would be rather charming if we weren't trying to catch someone," Cora mused. "Perhaps we could return another time?" She looked back at Adam, lowering her gaze in a slightly shy manner. Were her cheeks a bit pink as well? Strange. What reason could she have to feel embarrassed? Unless he'd done something awkward without realizing it, which was entirely possible.

To keep his mind on task, he turned toward the back of the boat, where the steam engine had been artfully draped with ferns. Maybe the leaves were supposed to resemble scales. They looked more like green feathers. Adam pushed a drooping frond out of the way and examined the machine.

He rocked back in surprise. "This engine is plenty powerful. This boat should go twice as fast, at least."

"Nope," the boatman replied. "Top speed. Sorry."

Cora drummed irritably on the side of the craft. "Maybe I should jump in and swim after him."

"No, no." Adam nudged her gently aside and bent down near the controls, running his fingers along an access panel, looking for a latch. "This must be speed limited. Somewhere under here…"

The panel popped open and the boatman jumped. "Hey! What do you think you're doing?"

Adam peered at the inner workings of the controls for a few seconds. "Ah. This." He reached in, grabbed a piece, and yanked. The speed limiter clicked off and the boat surged forward.

"Gah!" The captain cursed and jerked at the controls. "Are you out of your gosh-darned mind?"

"No, go, go," Cora urged. "We can catch him. Hurry! He looks like he's giving up and heading for the side of the basin."

"If he doesn't watch it, he's going to steer right into the cascades," the boatman snorted, but he pointed the now-speedier dragon at the lethargic swan. Adam guessed he was secretly enjoying the pursuit but couldn't admit to it.

With the speed no longer limited, the dragon boat swiftly closed in on its prey. Off to their left, water sprayed into the air from one of the cascade fountains, showering both boats with a fine but unrelenting mist. The reporter bumped his swan boat up against the concrete wall, shielding his camera from the moisture as he attempted to scramble up and out of the boat. The swan swayed, still hissing steam.

"Pull up right behind him and we'll hop out," Adam requested.

"Ram him!" Cora cried.

"Look, lady, this is my job. If I ruin the boat, I'm fired." The captain steered deftly alongside the wall. "Get out. And don't come back."

Adam hauled himself up onto the wall and over the rail. "We'll come back and pay! Promise!" He could at least be the Apologetic and Appreciative Lord of Chaos.

Cora vaulted over the rail beside him and broke into a run. Their enemy's lead had all but vanished. Cora flew at him with a speed fueled by her thirst for justice, launching herself and tackling him to the ground. Adam skittered to a halt beside them, blocking the clearest escape route in case the man regained his feet.

"Who are you?" Cora demanded.

The reporter shoved her roughly aside and began to rise. Adam stepped closer. The reporter held up a hand in a gesture of surrender.

"Okay, okay! Enough. I'm Roger Franklin. Journalist."

"Isn't that what you said when you accosted us at the Tyrolean Alps, claiming to be from the Post-Dispatch?" Adam demanded.

"I know, I know. I'm sorry. No one wants to give interviews if I say I write for the Daily Tattler."

Cora brushed off her skirts and glared up at Franklin. "And rightly so, you slandering lout!"

"Hey, I wrote the truth," Franklin protested. "Just livened it up a bit. He's at the center of a lot of mishaps you can't deny that."

"Who hired you?" Adam demanded. "Who set up all these 'mishaps'?"

One side of Franklin's mouth twitched. "AutomaTech."

Adam blinked in surprise. "Hampton?"

"And maybe that goon Rawley, but yeah. Comes from the top."

"But why? He fired me. What else does he want?"

"Ah." Franklin grinned. "This is where the story gets fun. They're out of money. Broke. Just this side of ruin. Spent a boatload on some failed airship project. Your machine was the only thing selling. Their plan for salvation? Discredit you so you can't sell it on your own, then market their own version in its place. And I'm going to write the whole story. So you see? I'm on your side."

"Hah!" Cora snapped.

"But…" Adam fidgeted with his spectacles. "I own the patent. Even if they duplicate the Electro-Flex, I'll get the licensing fee. They won't make any more than they're making now."

Franklin snorted. "Please. You think they're willing to destroy you and not willing to skirt the law? Claim their version is 'different'? But don't worry. When I've got all the info, I'm going to expose them to the world and watch them crash. It's a far better story than the misadventures of a nobody engineer. No offense."

"I'm offended," Cora muttered, crossing her hands beneath her breasts. Her dress was damp from their trip past the fountains, and the wet fabric clung to her. Adam looked hastily away.

"And you expect us to believe all this?" Adam asked Franklin. "After the way you ran?"

The reporter shrugged. "Look, I want the story, okay. I'm not in this to get killed or go to jail. I thought I could get away, but you two were more persistent than I expected. So, fine. You win. Your story wasn't the good one, anyway. Just an appetizer. Now let me go. You don't want to get in trouble with the law any more than I do."

Adam held out a hand. "Give me the camera."

"What? No!" Franklin clutched it to his chest. "I've got a photo of her punching that buffoon in the balls. I ain't giving that up for you."

"I'm not afraid of law enforcement, Mr. Franklin," Adam replied. "But given your involvement in the events of the past weeks, perhaps you should be. Give me the camera, or I'll take you right to the police." He glanced off to his right. "Starting with contacting that security guard over there."

There was no security guard, but Franklin panicked. "Fine, fine." He shoved the camera at Adam. Adam popped it open, pulled out the film, and then handed it back.

"Thank you."

Franklin took off running without another word.

"Damn," Adam swore. "I don't even know what to do other

than hope he was serious and he writes an article to expose them."

"Call the police." Cora's voice sounded tired. Adam whirled toward her. "Tell them everything. They'll at least be able to advise you." Her shoulders drooped and she rubbed her temple as if she had a headache.

"Cora, are you okay?"

"Tired. Suddenly all the excitement wore off and now..." She swayed and Adam grabbed her arm.

"You need to rest. I should never have let you run all around like that."

Her weary smile shot straight to his heart. "I'm glad you did. We hunted down a bad guy and solved a mystery. Together."

Adam stepped close to press a quick kiss to her cheek. "Yes, we did."

Cora let herself fall against his chest. "Take me home."

He lifted a hand to hail a passing carriage. She'd given him her all. Now it was his turn.

25

Excerpt of a letter from Miss Cora Maxwell to Mr. Adam Levett, dated October 29, 1903

Dear Mr. Levett,

Please excuse me if this letter is dusted in crumbs...

CORA WOKE TO A RUMBLING STOMACH. Her nose twitched at the scent of food as she scrubbed a hand over groggy eyes. How long had she been out? She hadn't napped that hard in years, if ever.

Slowly, she levered herself up on one elbow and surveyed the room. Adam sat at the desk, munching on a sandwich. A second plate of food sat beside his, untouched.

"Is that for me?"

"Ah, Cora, you're awake. Wonderful." He carried the plate to her and perched on the corner of the bed. "Ham with tomato and Swiss cheese, grilled to golden perfection and a salad of greens dressed with oil and vinegar."

Cora sat up straighter, rubbing her eyes again just to make sure she wasn't still dreaming. "How did you know that's my favorite?"

Adam grinned. "You told me. 'Dear Mr. Levett. Please excuse me if this letter is dusted with crumbs, but I am pressed for time and writing during lunch. I'm having my favorite,' etc. etc."

"You have quite the memory."

"Or maybe I read your letters too many times over." He gave her a bashful grin.

Cora slipped from the bed and padded over to the washstand, splashing her face with cool water and scrubbing her teeth before returning to the bed and her meal. She dug in eagerly.

"How are you feeling?" Adam asked. "Hungry, obviously."

She could only nod.

"Tired? Achy? Ill at all? Any lingering effects from the poison this morning?"

She shook her head.

"Good."

Cora swallowed her bite. "I'm still feeling slightly tired, but it's the sort a good night's sleep will take care of. I'll be ready for my next event in the morning."

She looked across the room to where her bow and arrows rested against the wall. She'd been so determined to help Adam she'd abandoned her equipment without a thought. Fortunately, she had friends she could rely on to help her out. *Where were they now*, she wondered.

Her answer came a few minutes later, when the door opened and Jane and Harriet entered. They immediately rushed to her side, both talking at once.

"I'm feeling much better," Cora responded to the barrage of questions about her health. "I'll finish my dinner and then turn in for the night."

She glanced down at her rumpled dress. Had Adam removed her boots and corset? She couldn't remember. She'd been so exhausted by the time they'd arrived here, nearly falling asleep in his arms.

"Excellent," Harriet said brightly. "Well, we just came to return your key." She placed the key on the washstand. "All our things are in our new room upstairs. I'm sure Mr Levett will see that you're undisturbed for the evening." She winked at Cora and started for the door.

Cora's mouthful of food prevented her from saying anything but a startled, "*Mmph.*"

"Good night. Sleep well." Jane waved. The two women vanished out the door.

Cora finished her bite and accepted a glass of water from Adam. "Did they just enable our illicit tryst?"

Adam's smile was feral. "I certainly hope so. If you're up for it."

"I have a condom."

He blinked. "You do? Where did you get that?"

"That man who was carrying on about the benefits of sexual activity before a competition," Cora answered. "He was passing them out and dropped one." She climbed out of bed and fetched the small packet from her personal effects. She passed it to Adam and resumed her dinner while he examined it.

"Wow. This is fabulous. I almost don't want to use it."

Cora speared a forkful of salad. "Open it carefully so we can save the wrapper as a souvenir. I feel as if it goes with this." She reached a hand to her hair, only to discover her brass flower missing. "Oh, no!"

"Don't panic, it's over atop the chest of drawers," Adam assured her. "I thought you wouldn't like for it to get damaged or thoroughly tangled in your hair."

Cora blew out a breath of relief. "Thank you."

"I guess you like it, then?"

"I love it." It was as close as she would go toward saying, "I love you," just now. Tomorrow she had a competition to win and then they had to follow up on the information they'd learned from Mr. Franklin. Only then could she take that great leap into the unknown. Risk their friendship for the possibility of something different.

Cora blushed, imagining herself and Adam sitting close during a lazy dragon boat ride, sharing one of those ice cream cones she had yet to try, or simply walking the fair, scandalously hand-in-hand. A real romance.

Tonight, though, they would be friends with perquisites one final time. She finished off her sandwich, then carried the empty plate to the desk.

"I think I'm ready for bed now."

Adam's gaze tracked hungrily up and down her figure. "Are you? You look overdressed to me."

Cora hiked up her skirt high enough to show off her stockings. "I could do something about that."

"No, no. Allow me." With one long stride he closed the distance between them, cupping her face in his hands and pressing a long, eager kiss to her mouth. "Ah, Cora," he sighed when they at last came up for air. "You were so magnificent today." His fingers worked at the buttons of her dress while his lips grazed her jaw. "Strong, determined, brave, kind. I am still in awe of the way you hunted down that self-serving reporter, all for me."

"Of course." She clutched his shirt, her legs becoming unsteady as her body gave itself over to the pleasure of his touch. "How could I not? What sort of friend would that make me?"

He slipped a hand inside her open bodice, kneading her breast, rubbing his thumb over her taut nipple. "I only know what kind of friend you are. Lovely. Kissable."

"Adam." She squirmed closer to him. "Please. Can we move to the bed?"

He nuzzled her neck. "So impatient. One might think we hadn't touched one another in a week." He helped her tug her dress off, then guided her to the bed, where he deftly removed her stockings and drawers. "Ah, my Cora."

Adam gazed down at her, the silvery flecks in his eyes glittering with desire. Cora's skin warmed beneath his fiery gaze. She was probably flushed, but she didn't mind. The way he looked at her made her heart leap with joy. He longed for her. He ached for her. He loved her.

Please, please let him love her.

"Today is the nineteenth, correct?" he asked.

Cora had to think hard before answering. "Uh, yes. Why?"

He tossed his vest aside, then pulled his shirt up and over his head. "I want to remember the day I finally got to fuck the most beautiful woman in existence."

Well, she was absolutely blushing now. And extremely aroused. She ogled his lean, hard body as he shed his trousers, carefully unwrapped the souvenir condom, and slid it on over his erection. Already her heart was beating fast. She licked her lips and reached out for him. It had been too long since he'd held her, skin-to-skin. Too long since she'd felt his intimate touch.

Adam climbed into her embrace, kissing and fondling her as he settled himself between her thighs. The weight of him above her caused a new tremor of excitement. In the outside world she strove to be the champion, always in control of a situation, but here she yearned to be conquered. Here, she could let all of life go and surrender to her pleasure. She could be his, absolutely and completely.

A long sigh of delight escaped her lips as Adam showered her body with kisses, stroking between her legs to ready her for his penetration. Cora arched into his hand, already feeling the climax building. She *was* ready. So ready.

She wanted to say something sultry and inviting to urge him on. Perhaps, "Come to me, darling," or, "Take me now." Instead, the only word she managed to get out was a long, throaty, "Oh."

And, oh, did she love him. These last days without him had driven her to the edge, and she could wait no longer. Her body strained toward his, yearning to take him into her body as deeply as she'd taken him into her heart.

Even without words, Adam seemed to understand. He adjusted his position and pushed into her, slowly at first, giving her time to adjust to the sensation.

"Oh," Cora moaned again, clutching at his shoulders and thrusting her hips upward. It was good, so unbelievably, unbearably good, and she needed more. Deeper, harder, faster.

He began to move, in and out, steadily increasing the speed, his fingers teasing her clit as he worked inside her, pushing her closer and closer to the breaking point.

All the muscles she'd trained and strengthened for years clenched as Adam moved inside her, twisting and tightening, begging for release. Cora could barely withstand the onslaught. She was going to explode. She would shatter into a million pieces and be forever destroyed. It would be exquisite.

I love you. The words danced in her head. *I want you. I need you. I love you.*

"Cora," Adam groaned. Perspiration glistened on his forehead, and his breaths came hard and fast. "My Cora." He pulled almost all the way out, then thrust deep.

Yes. I'm yours.

She couldn't respond, too swept away by the coming climax. A pleading whimper slid across her lips.

Yes, love, please. Please. *Take me. Come with me.*

Her fingers dug into his skin. His clenched in the sheets to either side of her, as if hanging on for dear life.

"You're all mine," he rasped, voice choked with emotion.

Groaning, he drove into her again, and she spasmed in ecstasy, her body teetering on the precipice of rapture. They were close. They were both so close.

Adam pounded into her, claiming her with every thrust and every strangled word. "Mine. Mine. Mine."

Cora cried out, clenching around him, swept away in a sudden flood of pure bliss. Adam jerked and trembled, clutching her against him as his whole body shook with the force of their shared orgasm.

Together, they floated down to earth, clinging to one another, chests heaving and hearts racing. That lovely sleepiness settled over her, and she nuzzled against him, wanting to curl into his arms and sleep the night away in the warmth of his embrace. He stroked her hair and covered her lips with tender kisses.

Words of love begged to burst free, but Cora choked them back, instead using gentle fingers and sweet kisses to express her feelings. Soon, she promised herself. Soon she would tell him. She would share her heart and trust him to cherish it.

They cleaned up quickly, then snuggled down together beneath the covers, hugging and kissing again. Cora's head spun with pure happiness. Whatever the future held, she would never forget this perfect moment.

"Goodnight, my glorious, darling friend," Adam murmured.

"Goodnight," Cora answered, yawning. Sleep was coming on fast, but she held it off for a few more precious seconds, basking in the glow of her love.

I'm yours, she thought. *I'm absolutely yours. And you are mine.*

26

Excerpt of a letter from Mr. Adam Levett to Miss Cora Maxwell, dated July 25, 1903

I love the name Electro-Flex. It has the perfect ring. A device of champions. I have no doubt, Miss Maxwell, that you are a champion.

Sept. 20

*A*DAM SCRAMBLED UP INTO the front row of the bleachers, red-faced and breathing hard, and squeezed himself into the empty seat between Doyle and Cora's friends. So much for the care he'd taken with his appearance this morning. His tie had come loose and he'd stepped in a puddle of *something* during his dash from the railway station. The muck was now splattered all up the left leg of his trousers.

"From the Indianapolis Archery Club: Miss Cora Maxwell," the loudspeaker crackled.

Cora turned toward the stands, caught Adam's eye, and gave him a smile, touching the brass flower in her hair. He grinned back.

Just in time.

Doyle nudged Adam. "What kept you?"

"Had to run to my hotel to change and pick something up. The train schedule was not especially favorable."

"Ah." Doyle smirked.

Adam winced. He'd as much as admitted to being with Cora last night. Though Jane and Harriet already knew, so it was hardly a secret. As long as the widespread public didn't suspect, she was safe from scandal.

He changed the subject. "And where were *you* yesterday? You missed the first event."

"Interviewing for new jobs. I'm done with AutomaTech. And we need to talk."

Adam nodded. The company's financial situation and its connection to the Lord of Chaos article still loomed over him. Even the smallest bit of information Doyle may have heard could shed more light on the situation.

"Later." He gestured at Cora. "After. I missed the announcements. How does this event work?"

"Double National Round," Doyle informed him. "Ninety-six arrows at sixty yards and forty-eight at fifty."

"Ninety-six?" Adam echoed. At the longest distance in the women's competition. Good Lord, that sounded exhausting. He'd been too busy racing to get here to be nervous, but now an unsettled flutter began in his gut. This was her chance. Her moment to shine. And he was terrified for her.

"Cora ate all the same things at breakfast as Harriet and I," Jane assured him from her place at his right. "She brought her own flask of water, and she's been careful to avoid touching anything except her own equipment. We won't have a repeat of yesterday."

"Good," Adam replied, though his belly still refused to settle.

Cora's first arrow caught the edge of the outer yellow circle, as did her second. Adam rubbed sweaty palms on his trousers.

That's it, love. Today is all you.

He'd seen her shoot from this distance when she'd challenged Thompson, but that had only been thirty arrows, and the wind was stronger today. Cora's third arrow hit the inner white ring and Adam winced. At least she hadn't missed the target the way several of the women had.

A hand settled on his shoulder.

"Sit back," Doyle urged, his tone gentle. "She'll be fine."

Adam tried to relax his muscles and focus on watching Cora. The errant shot hadn't fazed her. She loosed another arrow and hit the yellow for a third time. Her gaze flicked to the stands and she gave him a little nod, as if to say, *I've got this*.

One by one, the arrows flew. Cora took the lead early and grew it steadily. The swirling wind sent some shots awry, but she continued on, unflappable. The larger her lead became, the more Adam relaxed. Even as the event wore on and she began to tire, her focus never wavered. She lined up the next shot and let it fly.

Adam applauded every shot. He cheered and called her name during every pause in the action. Even if she fell apart, he'd be here for her and she'd know it.

During the break to move the targets to fifty yards, Doyle gave Adam a discreet nudge. "Hey."

Adam glanced at his friend. "What's wrong?"

"Rawley's here. And I think he's looking at us, not at the competition."

"That bastard," Adam muttered. A Lord of Chaos incident, here at Cora's competition? Of course they'd try something like that. They'd been trailing him and knew he'd be here. He took a cautious look around. Rawley stood just at the end of the bleachers, leaning on the rail. Adam tried to watch out of the side of his eye, but anything past the lenses of his spectacles was no more than a blur. He didn't dare stare openly.

His fists clenched, his earlier tension shoved aside by a blazing fury. How dare they do this here? How dare they put Cora's competition at risk, especially after what had happened yesterday? He pushed abruptly up out of his seat and stalked down the row toward Rawley, apologizing to the other spectators as he went.

"Levett," Rawley said smoothly. "Fancy meeting you here."

"What's your game?" Adam demanded. "I'm not going to let you ruin things for these ladies. Tell me what you want from me or get lost."

Rawley propped himself up with one elbow on the rail. "Dunno what you're talking about. I'm here to watch the competition."

"Fine." Adam leaned on the rail beside him. "We'll watch it together."

He ought to leave. If he walked away, Rawley would have to follow. They could take their Lord of Chaos mayhem elsewhere and Cora would be safe to finish the match. He would hate missing out on her victory, but it was a sacrifice he was willing to make.

Adam straightened up and was about to step away from the rail, when Cora turned and looked toward the stands. Her face went pale and she faltered.

No. Adam gripped the rail and waved, trying to catch her attention. The moment she spied him he visibly relaxed. She wanted him there. Needed him there. If he disappeared, she'd know something was wrong and panic. She'd abandon her competition to come to his rescue.

Never.

Adam wouldn't allow such a thing to happen. Not when Cora had worked her whole life to compete at such a prominent event. He couldn't abandon her and he couldn't explain the situation. He was trapped. He spun towards Rawley.

"What do you want from me? I'll do it."

Rawley's brow furrowed in confusion.

"You want me to cause a scene? You want to humiliate me? Dump three dozen toasters on me again? Make me crash a flying bicycle? Fine. Anything. You wait until this competition is over and I'll go along with whatever scheme you've got planned."

"You're outta your damn mind," Rawley grumbled.

"Or do you want money?" Adam dug in his pocket. "I'll pay you to go away."

A large shadow blotted out the sun over a portion of the athletic field, and Adam automatically looked up. Just northeast of the field, a massive, bright red dirigible was rising from the aeronautic concourse. The airship drifted ponderously toward the stadium.

"What is that?" he wondered.

"An airship," Rawley sneered.

Cora buried another arrow in the red ring. She wouldn't increase her lead with that shot, but she was holding steady. Adam glanced up at the oncoming dirigible. Photographers, perhaps? He'd heard that photographer Mrs. Jessie Tarbox Beals was receiving acclaim for her photos taken from a hot air balloon.

Drips of liquid trickling from the bottom of the ship caught Adam's eye. "Is that ship leaking something?" A soft chuckle from Rawley made him whirl around. "What is it? What's it doing? Make it stop."

Rawley took a step back, holding up both hands. "You want me to stop an airship? You're cracked."

"But you know what's happening. You and Hampton..." Adam choked on the words. "Oh, God. Is that his experimental firefighting airship?"

Rawley shrugged one shoulder. "Could be."

Adam gaped up at the dirigible. The prototype was more massive than he had expected. But every bit as sluggish and leaky as he would have predicted. If it dumped its cargo on the archers...

"Make it stop," he begged. "Signal them. Something. Anything."

"Look, Levett, I'm just here to make certain you don't run off."

A droplet splatted on Adam's head. The airship hovered low over the stadium, a fine mist spraying out in all directions from jets encircling the hull. Larger droplets seeped from the bottom.

A murmur ran through the crowd. On the field, the archers continued shooting.

Adam seized Rawley's wrist. "If this ruins her competition, I will personally see you all thrown in prison for the rest of your goddamned lives."

Rawley jerked away. "Good luck with that, Lord of Chaos."

The dirigible had come to a stop directly overhead, putting Cora and the first several rows of spectators beneath the worst of the leakage. Fans sprang from their seats, crying out as they hurried for drier ground. Several spectators jostled Adam as they raced by, but he didn't even turn to look. His fingers tightened around the rail, his attention fixed on Cora.

The competition ran on, uninterrupted, most of the archers not terribly bothered by the mist. Cora's location, though, was growing muddy, and water continued to spurt and occasionally stream down on her. The crowd, now almost entirely moved to drier ground, buzzed with nervous interest. Snippets of conversation reached Adam's ears.

"What *is* that?"

"…awful mess…"

"…think it's safe?"

"…stop the competition?"

Safely out of the way, several judges huddled, talking. One gestured at Cora. Another shrugged. Their expressions suggested bafflement, uncertainty, helplessness. One man flipped through what must have been a rule book. As if it had instructions for what to do in the event of a leaky dirigible.

A sudden gush of water drenched Cora and her arrow dug into the ground some ten feet short of the target. Adam's heart clenched. He was powerless to stop this. He had nothing to fight with. Nothing but his presence and his voice.

"Call a time out!" he shouted. The judges didn't respond, either because they couldn't hear him over the rumbling of the airship's engine and the splashing of water, or because they didn't care what a random fan thought.

Whatever the case, Adam couldn't assume they would halt the event. He hurried up into the now-empty stands, taking a seat as close to Cora as possible, ignoring the damp bench and his soggy clothing.

"I'm here, Cora!" he shouted. "You can do it!"

She turned toward him. Her dress was plastered to her body, and wet tendrils of hair framed her face. She nodded at him, nocked an arrow and shot. Blue circle. Not good, but not disastrous.

"I believe in you!" he continued. A cascade of water crashed down on them, soaking him to the skin and turning the ground at Cora's feet into a swampy mess.

She shot and shot, and still the ship hovered, dripping, spurting, interrupting her rhythm. Still the judges murmured, doing nothing. Adam stood alone in the front row, the only person remaining in the path of the deluge. The crowd continued to chatter, the words not quite intelligible. He knew what they were saying. He'd be in the papers. Probably Franklin or some other reporter was photographing him. Well, forget them. Forget the judges and the crowd and his enemies. This was him and Cora against the world, and the Lord of Chaos did not abandon his queen.

"Good shot, Cora!" he called, and she acknowledged him with a slight lift of her bow. She was going to do this. She was going to win, wet and bedraggled, her skirts caked in mud. "They can't stop you!"

Above him, the ship creaked and groaned. With a crack, a panel in the hull burst open, and water cascaded down, knocking Cora from her feet and sending another arrow far off target.

Adam cupped his hands around his mouth to make certain she could hear. "Whatever happens, you're my champion! You're *always* my champion!"

Cora clambered to her feet, defiantly taking up her stance again. She was his warrior, his goddess, and he would never leave her to fight alone.

He rose from his seat and shouted loud enough for the whole crowd to hear him, "I love you!"

27

Excerpt of a letter from Miss Cora Maxwell to Mr. Adam Levett, dated May 19, 1904

I'm so glad you'll be in St. Louis to see me! It will mean so much to have a supporter in the stands!

Much of Cora's lead had vanished during her struggles to avoid the deluge from that godforsaken dirigible, but she refused to dwell on that. She had ten arrows left, at only fifty yards, and though she was soaked to the bone and caked in mud, she intended to make these the ten best shots of her life. Because Adam was watching her. Because people were pointing and staring, whispering about him, but he wouldn't desert her. Because he was the truest fan anyone could wish for and he loved her.

Cora eyed the target, controlled her body and her breathing, pushed all worries to the side. Bullseye.

I love you, too.

Bullseye.

This is all for you.

The water from the dirigible was no more than a handful of

lingering droplets now. The ground squelched beneath Cora's feet, but she shifted her position and braced herself.

Aim, fire. Aim, fire. Four arrows left. Three. Two.

She released her final shot, watching the arrow zip toward the target, hearing the *thunk* as it stuck fast in the dead center of the target.

"I win," she declared.

An instant later, her knees gave out and she sank to the ground, exhausted.

The next thing she knew, Adam was at her side, wrapping his arms around her, helping her to her feet. Above them, the meddlesome airship floated slowly away, rising higher now that it was relieved of the weight of all the water.

"Olympic champion, with seven hundred thirteen points, Miss Cora Maxwell," a judge announced over the loudspeaker.

The same flying dragon from yesterday delivered a gleaming gold medal, and Cora allowed Adam to pin it to her ruined dress.

"You are everyone's champion," he said, beaming at her with the most glorious smile she'd ever beheld.

"I'm happy just being yours," she replied.

He leaned toward her, as if to kiss her, but people were still watching, and he'd been the object of more than enough attention already today. Cora stepped back.

"Let's go talk to everyone else," she said. "It looks like Doyle might be waiting for you."

They walked side-by-side to a drier portion of the field, where her friends waited along the rail. They were all damp, but looked to have avoided the worst of the mess, unlike herself and Adam. Doyle had a vice-like grip on the arm of a man she recognized as that scowling fellow from the AutomaTech booth.

"Cora, you were amazing!" Jane exclaimed, bouncing up and down. She flung her arms around Cora, not seeming to care that she came away with mud on her own clothing. Harriet hugged her too, and Benedict gave her a bow.

"Miss Maxwell, you are superb," Benedict said. "And clearly far too passionate for me. But I think perhaps Mr. Levett might be exactly your sort."

Adam's hand settled on the small of Cora's back. "I certainly hope so."

Doyle shoved his prisoner at Adam. "This scum has an apology to make to the both of you."

"Fuck off," the man snarled.

Adam calmly polished his spectacles on his wet sleeve, which probably did no good whatsoever. "I'm surprised at you, Rawley. Where did this loyalty to Hampton come from? I hope he hasn't promised you money."

Rawley started. "What do you mean?"

"He's broke. AutomaTech has no money."

"Bullshit."

"Not at all," Doyle cut in. "The other day I was researching current pay for new employees and the possibility of asking for a raise, and came upon some interesting rumors. Seems the company is falling behind on its payments. There's a freeze on hiring. Suppliers demanding money. Not good."

"Just like Mr. Franklin the reporter told us," Cora added. "You know him, I assume, Mr. Rawley?"

Rawley scowled. "Yeah, I know him."

"That airship was the final blow, I bet." Adam waved a hand toward the disappearing ship. "Hampton sank far too much money into a flawed design, trying to push it out in time for the fair. And all it did was fail."

"Quite publicly, too," Cora pointed out. "I'm sure Franklin has a fantastic story in mind. One about how AutomaTech nearly ruined an Olympic event." She gave Rawley a sugary smile. "If you tell us what you know, maybe we'll ask him to keep your name out of it."

"Conniving bitch," he muttered. "Yeah, Hampton hired

him. He and I followed you around. I used Hampton's stupid dragons to cause trouble."

"Why Cora?" Adam demanded. "Why poison her? Disrupt her events? What did she ever do to you, you scum?"

Rawley snickered. "Nothing. But you'd vanished. Hampton figured going after the girl would draw you out. And here you are. The poison was that Thompson fellow's idea. He did it just for fun. Hates her."

"The feeling is mutual," Cora muttered.

"Mr. Rawley!"

Cora turned to find Mr. Franklin running toward them, his clothes irritatingly dry, pencil and notepad in hand. "If you give me an exclusive interview of all you know, I promise to refer to you only as a 'trusted source.'"

"And not go to the police," Rawley insisted.

"And that." Franklin motioned with his head. "Let's talk. Congratulations, Miss Maxwell. I hope the rest of you enjoy your day."

"Well, that's that, I suppose," Doyle remarked as the other men departed. He clapped Adam on the shoulder. "No more fame for you. All the talk will be about Miss Maxwell's stunning victory and the collapse of AutomaTech. I'll leave you all to clean up. I'm going job hunting. Hoping for an interview with Tagget Industries while Tagget himself is in town. Did you hear he won the road car race even though he stopped to give a couple of people a ride?"

Adam and Cora grinned at one another. "Imagine that," Adam chuckled.

"I know, right? Shall we meet for dinner?"

Cora rolled her shoulders, suddenly feeling the full weight of her sodden clothing. "Not tonight, thank you. I'm taking a long, hot bath, eating in my room, and spending the rest of the day in bed. Mr. Levett, would you be kind enough to escort me home?"

"Of course." He took her arm and they bade goodbye to their friends.

"All day in bed, hmm?" he asked when they were alone. "May I join you?"

Cora grinned. "Only if you promise to ravish me again."

His answering smile was radiant. "How could I not? Clearly the pre-competition ravishment is effective, and you *do* have the team event remaining tomorrow."

Cora leaned close to him, letting her head fall onto his shoulder. "I knew I could count on you."

28

Excerpt of a letter from Mr. Adam Levett to Miss Cora Maxwell, dated June 27, 1904—unsent

To be blunt: I love you.

Sept. 21

ADAM APPLAUDED—from the stands this time—as Cora cheerfully accepted a silver medal. The outcome of this event had never been in doubt. With only six ladies competing, four from the Cincinnati Archery Club, Cora had been paired with a woman from Washington, D.C. to make up a two-person second team. Their runner-up spot had been guaranteed.

But the results hardly mattered to any of the women. Cora had shot brilliantly, everyone had enjoyed the event, and nothing untoward had occurred. It was a peaceful, happy ending to a wild Olympic championship.

Wearing her full array of medals, Cora skipped joyfully to her little cluster of fans, accepting hugs from her friends and a kiss on the cheek from Adam.

The sun streamed down on the Exposition today, but even its warm glow was no match for Cora's radiance. Today was perfect. Today he would take his chance, spill his heart, and hope for the best.

Adam had originally intended to take her out last night for a celebration, but after the chaos and the mud, he'd put it off. This would be better. No worries, no pressure, just happiness.

"Excuse me, Miss Maxwell?" called a voice with a distinct Northeastern accent. A young man walked toward them, clutching a notebook. He wore a cap, no coat, and bright red suspenders over his gray vest. "Bruce Caldwell, Boston Herald," he introduced himself. "I've been covering the Olympic games here for two months, and this is my last event. I'd be honored if I could conclude my articles with an interview with the most tenacious archer in the Games."

Cora's face glowed with delight. "I would love to be in your paper. Thank you!"

Adam sat down on the bleachers to wait, while Cora chatted about her entire Olympic experience, from training to today's event. Her hands waved as she talked and her smile was as wide as the ocean. She left nothing out, whether a struggle or a triumph, and she praised both her fellow competitors and all the women athletes who had gone before her. Adam even got a mention himself, when she brought up the Electro-Flex and how vital it had been to her rehabilitation.

Mr. Caldwell listened attentively, smiling the entire time. This would be a good, fair article, and Adam couldn't wait to read it. Somehow, he'd have to get his hands on a Boston newspaper.

"Tell Cora we'll see her at dinner this evening," Harriet whispered in Adam's ear. "We're all off to explore. Enjoy your afternoon together." She winked at him before walking away. It seemed everyone knew he was planning something.

Which meant Cora probably knew, too. Butterflies flew madly about in his stomach. She'd yet to declare that she loved him, though he believed she did. Last night after they'd made love she'd told him, "And you're mine, too. Don't forget it."

He wouldn't. Not ever. His heart was one hundred percent hers. If for any reason she still preferred to remain friends rather than something more romantic, he would accept that, but he needed her to know how he truly felt.

"Ready to take that ride on the Ferris wheel at last?" he asked, when Mr. Caldwell departed with a tip of his cap.

"Absolutely. And if it breaks down, even after the AutomaTech mischief has been exposed, we'll know you're simply cursed." She gave him an impish smile.

"It won't break," he replied, though his churning gut disagreed.

Adam bought their tickets with a shiny silver dollar, but instead of joining the line waiting to board the next car, he pulled Cora aside.

"Is the wedding car rented now?" he asked a man directing traffic.

"I don't think so."

"Good. We'd like to wait for it to come around."

The man gave Adam an exasperated look. "I suppose."

Cora gripped Adam's hand and gave it a squeeze. A giddiness swept over him, an excited anxiety now, and slightly less terrifying. *Yes. We are one of* those *couples. Excessively romantic.*

A full rotation only took twenty minutes, and soon enough Adam and Cora were stepping into the decorated car for their ride to the top of the world. Adam could imagine music rising from the piano, the scent of flowers, a minister saying, "Dearly beloved…" How he managed not to drop to his knees immediately, he'd never know.

While he fretted in silence, Cora talked, pointing out all the buildings she recognized from their walks around the fair. Adam fidgeted, wiping his spectacles so many times they were probably cleaner than when he'd gotten them.

When at last the car stopped at the very top, he dug his special surprise from his pocket and went down on one knee.

"Cora, darling," he began. She turned toward him, but then glanced back at the scenery behind her. Damn. Had he messed this up? He'd thought the top would be the most romantic. Not knowing what else to do, he plowed ahead. "I loved you even before I met you. I loved your spirit, your humor, your determination. Now, every day we're together I only love you more."

"Stop," she interrupted.

Adam's heart skipped a beat. She didn't want this. He'd ruined everything.

"You're missing the world."

Huh?

Cora grabbed him by the arm and hauled him to his feet, pushing him to the rail to look out over the city and beyond.

"Don't miss it for me." She leaned against him, her arm slipping around his waist. "I want you to see everything. I want us to see it together."

Adam wrapped his arm around her shoulder, holding her close. "Together, then. Wherever life takes us, if you'll have me."

Her head fell onto his shoulder. "Tell me again the part about loving me."

"I'll always love you, Cora. As a friend, as a lover, and hopefully as a husband. I want to cheer your every victory. I want to join your adventures. And I desperately need your input on my sporting machines."

She laughed. "I want those things too. I love you. I *know* I love you. When I finally realized it, I got this feeling so deep inside that this was right. It was real. Every competition, everything, will always be for you. For us together."

The wheel began to rotate again, and Adam brandished his secret weapon: a small brass ring taken from the broken Electro-Flex.

Cora gasped. "Is that—"

"You dream about a proposal with the Electro-Flex, you

get a proposal with the Electro-Flex." He brushed a quick kiss across her lips. "Besides, it brought us together. I hope it will keep us that way. Will you marry me?"

Cora's hand flew to her mouth, smothering a sob. Tears streamed down her cheeks. She held out her hand to allow him to slip the ring onto her finger.

"S-sorry," she choked. "I m-meant to say, 'yes.'"

Adam just held her, his own eyes misting over. He pressed a kiss into her hair. "Now do you think we might miss a bit of the world?"

She answered by winding her arms around him and kissing him with absolute abandon. Never in his life had he ever tasted anything sweeter than her. His Cora.

When they paused to catch their breath, she cupped his cheek with one hand, smiling up at him. "This means we won't be friends with kissing anymore. We'll have to call ourselves something else."

"Oh? What did you have in mind?"

Her green eyes twinkled. "Friends for as long as we both shall live."

EPILOGUE

Sept. 19, 1905
Indianapolis, Indiana

"Mrs. Levett, Mrs. Levett, did you see?" The girl bounced up and down, pointing at the target where she had just hit her first bullseye.

"I did see. It was a beautiful shot," Cora congratulated her. "Can you tell me what you did that time that made it so accurate?"

The girl pursed her lips in thought. "Um, well, I was paying attention to my bow and the target and not what anyone else was doing."

"Important," Cora agreed.

"And I stood with my feet like this and my hands like this." She demonstrated her stance.

"Excellent."

"And I think I was trying hard, but not too hard."

Cora nodded. "You were concentrating, but your body was relaxed. Every time you shoot you get a little bit more comfortable doing it. You want it to become so natural that it will be the same every single time. Let's try it again and see how close you can come to repeating that shot."

The girl shot again, making a good shot but not quite enough to match.

"Good," Cora said. She made a small adjustment to the girl's grip. "Shoot the rest of the arrows in your quiver and see how many good shots you can get. Once they're near the center every time, you'll be ready to try a longer distance." She left the girl to continue practicing and moved on to the next student.

Her archery school was small, but growing, and teaching brought her a sense of satisfaction. She was making a difference to the next generation of women athletes. Encouraging dreams. Maybe one of these girls would win a gold medal of her own some day.

A sensation of being watched prickled at the back of her neck, and she turned to find her husband leaning in the doorway, arms crossed over his chest. How long had he been there? Her indoor range and his workshop shared a building: an old warehouse they'd bought for cheap and fixed up to suit their needs. The funds had come almost entirely from sales of the Electro-Flex, which had experienced a surge in popularity following mentions in both the Boston Herald and the Daily Tattler. Throughout the year, they'd added several more products to the AthleTech brand.

Cora gave Adam a wave and returned to her teaching, reminding the girls to make certain no one was shooting before retrieving their arrows and supervising the storage of their equipment. This group no longer needed much help. Thinking back on their progress over the last several months made her heart swell with pride.

"Good day?" Adam asked, walking up to give her a hug.

"Yes. I love how much they've improved and how much fun they're having. This is what sport is really all about: exercising your mind and your body and enjoying it."

"And learning the importance of perseverance, discipline,

and teamwork." He nuzzled her neck, sucking on her skin just hard enough that it might leave a love mark. "You and I are quite the experts at teamwork."

Cora sighed in response.

"Would you like to go out to dinner tonight, or do you prefer to stay in and cuddle?"

"Go out?" Cora wondered. "What's the occasion? Did you sell another invention?"

"Mmm." His arms tightened around her. "It's our anniversary. One of them, anyway."

Adam's hands had begun running up and down her body, and Cora had to concentrate hard to process his words. "My first Olympic event?"

"And after. Remember? Us. A bed. 'Most beautiful woman in existence'?"

"Oh." Cora's cheeks flamed as excitement shivered through her body. "I'm afraid I don't have any Olympic condoms today."

"We don't need one if we want to expand our family. We can, if you'd like. Our business is small, but stable."

"True," Cora murmured, considering it. She leaned into him, inhaling the scent of freshly laundered clothing and shaving soap. She tilted her chin up and he kissed her, slowly, lovingly, as if he were content to kiss her until the end of time.

"I think we might have to head home," he gasped.

Cora grinned at him mischievously. "Or we could have a quick bit of fun on the archery range and then go to dinner afterward, when we are hungry from our sport."

Adam ground his hips against her. Seemed he liked the idea. "That would be fitting."

Cora splayed her hands across his chest, popping open the buttons of his vest. "How so?"

"Obviously you are descended from Eros himself," Adam explained. "You may think all you did was write me a letter one summer day, but in truth, you fired your love dart at me."

She smiled up at him, loving him. Loving them. "Was it a good shot?"

He took hold of her hand and placed it directly above his heart. "Bullseye."

THE END

POSTLUDE

Sept. 22, 1904
The Palace of Luxene

"CLEANING RATS for home and office!"

The small metal creature darted past Evan's feet to suck up the glob of ice cream.

"Tagget original design! Trusted since 1879!"

The rat scampered off, leaving a sticky trail in its wake. Evan cursed under his breath and bent to catch the creature as it ran by. Melted ice cream oozed from every gap in its body. Evan held the slimy, wriggling thing at arm's length to keep the foul mess as far from his suit as possible.

"You do realize that the rats need to be emptied periodically?" he asked the salesman, dangling the rat in front of his face.

"Uh…"

"Allow me to demonstrate." Evan snapped the shell off the rat and dumped the contents onto the floor at the salesman's feet. He turned the sticky creature over in his hands, shaking his head. "Terribly shoddy construction," he sighed. "Thin metal. Poor welds." He snapped the rat back together and set it down on the floor, where it immediately began to ingest the ice cream it had been relieved of.

"Highest quality," the salesman recited, clearly not knowing anything about the rat except what he'd been taught to say. "Tagget original design."

Evan sniffed. "No. The legs are attached at the wrong angle, it has no sensor to indicate when the chamber is full, and my original design used a wind-up key because luxene wouldn't be discovered for another decade."

The salesman gaped at him. "I-I—"

"I suggest you look for a new job," Evan said coolly. "Your employer and their cheap, unauthorized copies are not going to enjoy hearing from my lawyers. Have a nice day." He walked off, ruining a perfectly good handkerchief as he tried to wipe away the last of the ice cream residue.

Revolting. Now he needed to wash his hands and call his lawyers, when he would have preferred to be racing his motorcar or playing with machines in his workshop. Sometimes he wondered why he bothered with all this business nonsense.

"Mr. Tagget, sir!" called an employee from the Tagget Industries booth a short distance ahead. Her face was curved in a wide smile. "Good news, sir. Sales are booming. Up three percent more this week."

Ah, yes. That was why he bothered. He would never lack for money. Never, ever again.

· · · ⚯ · · ·

See more of Evan in *Eden's Voice*, *Sass and Steam* Book 1, available at your favorite retailer.

And learn how he gets his own Happily Ever After in *Priceless*, *Sass and Steam* Book 2, available November 20, 2020.

₼ISTORICAL NOTE

The Louisiana Purchase Exposition in St. Louis, Missouri, ran from April 30th to December 1st, 1904, and was visited by more than nineteen million people over the course of that time. People flocked to St. Louis to entertain themselves with thrill rides, art, music, and new and unusual foods. The fair allowed people to experience cultures from around the world and to see exciting new technologies for the first time.

It is important to note, however, that Cora and Adam's story is meant to be lighthearted and fun, and the portion of the 1200 acre fair they experience does not include the problematic side of the event.

Many of the Exposition exhibits were deeply steeped in colonialism and arranged in such a way as to promote a pseudo-scientific, racist world view. Thousands of indigenous people from around the world were brought to the fair for the anthropological exhibits, where they were mistreated and gawked at like zoo animals.

David Francis, former Missouri governor and one of the primary organizers of both the World's Fair and the Olympic Games, professed a desire for the fair to be unsegregated and inclusive, but despite his wishes the fair was plagued with racism. People of color reported being turned away from attractions and restaurants, and water fountains and spectator seating eventually did become segregated.

The Olympic Games, originally intended to be held in Chicago, were merged with the World's Fair when fair organizers threatened to hold their own athletic contests. Out of the seventeen disciplines and ninety-four events, only archery included women. Six women competed, all from the United States.

Cora's archery prowess is inspired by archer Matilda "Lida" Scott Howell, who easily won gold in both individual events and led the gold-medal winning team in the third event. While the women's events maxed out at a shorter distance than the men's events, if you compare the scores in the overlapping 50 yard and 60 yard distances, Mrs. Howell's scores are competitive with those of the top male contestants. By the time she retired from competition in 1907, she had competed in twenty national championships, winning seventeen of them. Her record scores stood until 1931.

About the Author

Award-winning author Catherine Stein believes that everyone deserves love and that Happily Ever After has the power to help, to heal, and to comfort. She writes sassy, sexy romance set during the Victorian and Edwardian eras. Her stories are full of action, adventure, magic, and fantastic technologies.

Catherine lives in Michigan with her husband and three rambunctious girls. She loves steampunk and Oxford commas, and can often be found dressed in Renaissance festival clothing, drinking copious amounts of tea.

· · · ⟶ · · ·

Visit Catherine online at
www.catsteinbooks.com
and join her VIP mailing list for a free short story.

Follow her on Twitter @catsteinbooks,
or like her page on Facebook @catsteinbooks.

Also by Catherine Stein

The Earl on the Train

An earl with a problem.
A woman with a plan.
The journey of a lifetime.

How to Seduce a Spy

A barmaid with a rare talent.
A spy on a mission.
A love neither can resist.

Not a Mourning Person

A determined widow.
An ancient curse.
Crime and passion.

Once a Rake, Always a Rogue

He's mended his ways.
But the woman he can't forget...
Might be his undoing.

Eden's Voice

Football, mechanical dragons,
industrial espionage, sexy romance.
Welcome to fall in Ann Arbor.

The Scoundrel's New Con

He's pulling the con of a lifetime.
Unless she exposes the naked truth.

Available at your favorite online retailer.

Thank you so much for reading.
If you enjoyed the book and are so inclined, I would love for
you to leave a review. Happy readers make an author's day!

I love hearing from readers,
so feel free to contact me on social media, or email:

catherine@catsteinbooks.com